Aunt Fanny

More Mittens

Aunt Fanny

More Mittens

1st Edition | ISBN: 978-3-75237-890-0

Place of Publication: Frankfurt am Main, Germany

Year of Publication: 2020

Outlook Verlag GmbH, Germany.

Reproduction of the original.

MORE MITTENS

BY

AUNT FANNY

A LETTER

FROM AUNT FANNY.

My Darling Children:

I wrote these stories, as I have already told you, some years ago, and took a great deal of pains with them. I called them "Life Among the Children;" when, lo and behold! somebody else had written a book with the very same name, but very different stories, and I never knew one word about it.

You may believe how sorry I was to take this pretty title when it belonged to another; and I was very thankful that I could get at the printer and have it changed.

What do you think of "The Doll's Wedding" for a name? I like it very much, because "Lily," whose dolls were married, is one of my particular pets; and what I have related, took place precisely as you read it. Lily is a funny darling; she had a "doll's regatta" once, and I do believe, in my next book, I will tell you all about it.

Meanwhile, if you will only laugh and grow fat as Lily does, and above all, try to be good and lovely as Maggie the Child Heroine is, I will write stories to interest you until my fingers feel as if they were all thumbs; for that is just how they *do* feel when they are very tired.

I wish I knew you all. I believe about three hundred children call me "Aunt Fanny" now, but I have room in my heart for *ever, ever* so many more. You see I have a patent elastic heart; and when you would think it was so crowded that a small doll could not squeeze in, if you only try, you would find there was plenty of room for *one more*, and that one would be you.

I wish good Mr. Somebody would make a telescope on purpose for me, powerful enough to see all the darling children at once. Fancy how perfectly delightful to see every little innocent child in the world with one eye!

Oh! that thought has quite upset me, laughing and thinking about it. So many little smiling faces at once—a great deal better than staring at the man in the moon, who has no expression at all worth talking about.

When I get it I will invite you all to come and take a peep at yourselves.

Good-by! I blow you a hundred kisses; and I hope the breeze is fair, so you will get them all safe and warm from your loving

AUNT FANNY.

THE DOLL'S WEDDING.

ONE day, Alice came home from school, and opening her drawer, to put away her things, she saw a letter lying on the very top of a pile of pantalets.

"Why, who can this be for?" said she, in a tone of delighted surprise. "Is it for me, mamma?"

"Yes," said her mother, "and it is sealed up so tight, that I expect it is of the greatest importance; perhaps from the President of the United States, requesting you to come to Washington immediately, to dine with him."

"Dear me, how delightful!" exclaimed Alice. "I like getting a letter, it's so very *oldy*, you know—just like grown people; did you pay the postman?" and in her impatience and excitement, she tore the envelope all to pieces. "Now read it, mamma, please," and then she began to jump up and down, and ended by turning a summerset on the bed.

Her mother laughed, and said: "If that is the way you are going to behave, when you go to see the President, I think he will be slightly astonished; but let us see, first, if he wrote it," and she read thus:—

"DEAR ALICE—

"My doll is to be married on next Friday, at two o'clock; and I should be very happy to see you, and as many dolls as you can bring.

"Yours, truly,

LILY.

"WEDNESDAY, Oct. 20th, 1858."

"Isn't it too nice!" cried Alice, with a joyful little scream. "A wedding!" and she bounced into a rocking-chair, and nearly tipped over backwards. "Dear me! what a *leany*-back chair! I very nearly upset. I'll take Anna with me; but she must have a new dress immediately—and a hoop petticoat; and, oh, mamma! her hands are all to pieces; the cotton is sticking out in every direction; can't you buy her a new pair? these old brown ones will never do to go to a wedding. Oh, dear! I am so glad," she continued, clapping her hands, "I won't have any trouble with her hair, because it is made of china, and I

4

need not put it up in curl-papers, as I did that poor old thing's in the corner, staring at me so crossly, just because I cut her nose off: she can't go to the wedding; she would frighten the bride into fits."

And now Alice ran off, and coaxed her sister, who was the very best sister in the whole world, or any where else, to make Anna a dress, grand enough for the occasion; and, thereupon, commenced a great rummaging in the rag-bag, and among their mother's stock of old ribbons; and in a short time Anna was made to look perfectly beautiful. The hoop petticoat gave her an appearance extremely like a balloon; and she had to sit down very carefully, to prevent it from going up in the air, and almost over her head.

When Friday came, it rained; and Alice's sister very kindly went to see if the wedding would come off, rain or shine. She came back with the information, that it would not take place if it rained; the ceremony would be postponed to the first fair day—a mode of proceeding rather unusual, but, I think, very sensible; and, I have no doubt, that *real live* people would be very glad to do the same; for some find it difficult to feel very happy when the rain is pouring down from the great black clouds.

Alice waited impatiently until Saturday. At first it was cloudy; but towards twelve o'clock the sun shone bright and warm, and Alice and her doll were soon dressed; the first, all smiles, doing every thing with a hop, skip and jump; while Miss Anna, whose heart, if she had any, was as hard, no doubt, as her china head, kept the same prinking smile on her face, as she was violently twisted and twitched about, and pins run into her in all directions; not to speak of her being thrown so hastily on the bed, while Alice was having her bonnet tied and her gloves put on, that she fell over on the top of her head, and remained in this painful position a quarter of an hour.

And now, all was ready, and kissing every body, even the cat, for "good-bye," Alice set out, with her sister and Miss Anna, for the scene of the festivities.

When they arrived, they found they were the very first, and were received with great ceremony by Lily.

"Dear me, Alice," she said, "we were obliged to have the ceremony yesterday, for so many little girls came we did not like to disappoint them; but there is to be a reception to-day."

"A reception! what's that?" said Alice.

"Why, the bride will see all her friends. I will tell you about the ceremony that took place yesterday, then you will know every thing. Shall I?"

"Oh, do!" cried Alice; "have it over again, can't you?"

5

"Oh, no! that would not do," said Lily. "Well, we put the bride and groom in the middle-room, leaning against the door; and, as the minister could not stand up alone, I tied him fast to a chair; he did not speak loud: so it was a kind of tableau."

"Oh!" said Alice, "what's that?"

"Why, like a picture, my dear;" said Lily, who was two years older than Alice, and of course knew a great deal more. She made all her explanations with sweetness and good-nature. She did not say, "Pooh! don't you know that?—what a goose!" as some children do. She had been taught true politeness by her dear mother, and every one who knew Lily loved her dearly.

"Just think, Alice," said Lily, "when the doors were opened, every body burst out laughing at the groom. Now, please don't you make a face or laugh;" and Lily opened the door leading into the reception-room, and Alice and her sister burst out laughing, too,—they could not help it; for—though the bride was a splendid lady, with a tarlatan dress and thread-lace veil—the groom—who was no less than the Count de Morny—was a knit-worsted doll, most dismal to behold. His brown-worsted wig not being finished on the top, he had to keep his cap on before all the ladies. His eyes were made of steel beads, sewed close together; one was perfect, but half of the beads had dropped out of the other, making him look as if he were winking at the company. He wore white-worsted mittens, black pantaloons, and a fiery red jacket. His nose was made by sewing the middle of his face into a hard knot, and it was a nose of a shape never before seen on this earth: and, altogether, the poor Count de Morny looked very much like a monkey with the toothache; and must have known it, for he hung his head as if he were ashamed of himself.

And now Lily set up the count and his bride on the sofa, with the minister on her other side—all, in great state and dignity, ready to receive the company.

They arrived very fast; and, before long, fourteen little girls, and three little boys—the only live gentlemen of the party,—and about twenty dolls were assembled.

When they were ushered into the reception-room, and saw the comical-looking groom, there was such a peal of merry, childish laughter that you would have thought the room was full of singing-birds—such little rollicking trills and carols, it was perfectly delightful to hear them. But Lily, with a very solemn and grave air, said, "Ladies, the groom is not of a very *prippersessing* appearance, but (as Mr. Curtis told me to say) he has a great deal of money."

This made the children laugh more than ever. What did they know or care about money? You might as well have talked Latin to those innocent little ones, as to try to make them believe that any body was any better for the money they had. No! that sort of belief is for "children of a larger growth."

And now Lily took up each little girl, in turn, and introduced her and her dolls to the bride. When Alice went, she did not know exactly what to say; but she recollected what the gentlemen on last New Year's day said to her mother, and she thought that would do nicely; so, dropping a pretty little courtesy, she pressed the white-kid hand of the bride, and, as a blush mantled in her cheek, she said, "How do you do? I wish you many happy returns of the season!" by which Alice meant, I suppose, that she ought to be married every year. At any rate, it was thought a very fine speech, and was imitated and repeated several times.

I must describe Rosalie's doll. Remember, dear little reader, this is all true. Well, Rosalie had a beautiful doll, dressed in a white tarlatan, covered all over with spangles, and trimmed with scarlet. She had an elegant bouquet of flowers on the waist, called a *corsage*, and the most splendid cut-glass diamonds on her wrists and shoulders. Rosalie's doll was decidedly the belle of the party.

There was a little girl present that was in what Lily called "a peck of troubles," for she had had no idea that it was to be such a grand affair, and she had brought her doll in a plain, white dress, rather tumbled, and, what was worse, barefooted. Just to think—a lady at a party without stockings or shoes! If she had been alive, instead of being made of china, I am sure she would have fainted.

When Lily saw Bertha's distress, she said, "I will lend your doll a pair of shoes, and she can be a lady from the other side of the Mississippi, where they are not so particular;" and little Bertha's face brightened into happiness again.

Lily handing Bertha her Doll, after lending the Shoes.

Jessie, a sweet little blue-eyed fairy, with quiet, gentle manners, brought two beautiful dolls, dressed in white, trimmed with black velvet. The children all kissed the dolls, they thought them "so sweet;" but Lily's mother kissed Jessie, and I think she had the best of it.

Ellie had a dolly that ought to have married the Kentucky giant, for she was so big she had to have a whole chair to herself. The dear little girl was so anxious to have her appear to advantage that, before she came to the party, she went with her brother into the garden, and, after a grand consultation, they picked two immense dahlias, which she insisted should be pinned on dolly's shoulders, and her mother had great difficulty in persuading her that dolly looked much handsomer without them.

Hugh, a dear little boy with very bright eyes, brought a boy-doll, which he called Mr. Brown.

There was one *live* doll at the party. She was not quite as high as Ellie's doll, and such a sweet little blue-eyed creature, with such soft, curling hair that, if she had not been jumping and laughing nearly all the time, you would really have taken her for a beautiful wax doll. Her name was little "Mary," and she was about two years old.

I wish you could have heard little Mary sing "Where is my little Kitty gone," sitting in a tiny chair with her little doll in her arms, bobbing it up and down in her lap to keep time. Her sweet little baby voice was like a robin's note; and I, for one, would not have lost that dear little song for all the Italian operas from here to China.

There were a great many other pretty children, and splendid dolls that I have no time to describe; and the bride and groom sat on the sofa and stared at them all, as if they never meant to look at any thing else.

And now that all had congratulated the happy couple, you would have thought that the queen of fun and frolic had joined the party, and all the cross children had gone up to the moon, and never meant to come down again; for the children—putting the dolls on the chairs, to play grown people—all tumbled down on the carpet, and had a grand game of "hunt the slipper," and did not leave off till supper was announced.

Supper was set out in—hem!—in the garret; but, let me tell you, it is quite as fine to go up so high to supper, as to dive down in the basement; at all events the children thought so, for they scuffled and scrambled up the stairs, all laughing and talking, and nobody listening, so that they might as well have given their ears to their dolls, for any use they were, and arrived at the festive banquet quite breathless.

And now, what a splendid sight presented itself! The table was beautifully ornamented, and brilliantly lighted by four candles about as long as your finger, one at each corner; in the centre was a large wedding cake, at least as big round as a breakfast plate, with roses and lilies and daffadowndillies all over it, perfectly beautiful to look at, and perfectly delicious to eat; and there was every thing else on the table that you can think of.

All the dolls were set up stiff and straight on one side, and the children on the other, and the children eat for both sides, and had the most delightful time, till the minister, who was a wax doll with short hair and movable eyes, was discovered to be fast asleep, or else his eyes had been accidentally put out—and, as the candles were also going out, it was high time for supper to be over.

The children now came down stairs, and, before they left, were invited by Lily to inspect the presents.

"Oh, dear!" cried Alice, "what a splendid silver cake-basket! and here is a knife, fork, and spoon, and, goody! just see these other spoons, with her name on them, how very *arittoscratic*."

Between you and me, little reader, the basket, and knife, fork and spoon, were silver—made of pewter; but there were, besides, six "darling little spoons," that were really silver, which had been given to Lily by her aunt; and Lily had presented them to her doll, the bride.

"And only see this china basket," said little Jessie; "blue basket and red handle; how perfect!"

"And who gave her the splendid embroidered pincushion, I wonder," said Alice, jumping up and down; "it will hold a whole row of pins, I'm sure; and

9

the beautiful preserve dishes, they would hold one cherry apiece; dear me! how nice they look!"

"They are salt-cellars," answered Lily, laughing, "and this is a china candlestick. I shall have to have some candles made, the size of knitting needles; but, dear me, ladies! just look at the groom! He must be going crazy!"

The children all turned to look, and there was the Count de Morny tumbled over on the sofa with his legs up in the air.

"What conduct!" cried Lily; "he ought to be ashamed of himself," and she marched up to the sofa, and took the bride's hand and boxed the Count's ears well, saying that "boxing ears was very much practised, since Queen Victoria had set the fashion."

And now it was getting late, for the sun's rays were coming red and aslant into the room, and all the little ones gathered up their dolls, and prepared to leave this delightful party.

I should think there were about two hundred kisses exchanged on this occasion; for everybody kissed everybody, and then everybody kissed Lily and the bride; and Lily kissed everybody else, and nobody kissed the Count de Morny, which was quite as many kisses as he deserved, for he was a perfect scarecrow, and nothing else; you might as well have tried to fish the moon out of the river, as expect him to sit up straight, and behave himself, or do any thing but wink and blink, and tumble over on his ugly old nose.

After the kissing, everybody said good-bye, and all the children went home delighted, to tell their parents of the nice time they had had; and they all hoped that Lily would soon take it into her dear little head, to invite them to another doll's wedding, as she had about a dozen dolls, and more paper dolls than she could count. Be sure, if she does, I will give you a faithful account of the whole affair.

WHAT CAME OF GIPSYING;

OR,

Think before you Act.

I ONCE knew a bright-eyed, handsome boy, with curling brown hair, which he had a habit of throwing, with a quick jerk of his head, back from his forehead; and this habit was a sort of type of his character, for he was so impetuous, that he would act upon an idea the very moment it came into his head, and this want of reflection led him into innumerable scrapes—some of them pretty serious.

"Charlie," said his father to him one day, "if you expect to get sugar plums and amusing story books in your Christmas stocking, instead of a birch rod, you must mend your ways considerably. How will you get along when you grow up to be a man, if you rush about the world like a comet, upsetting every thing in your way, and doing all manner of imprudent things without stopping to think twice?"

"Well, now, dear papa, I really will try to think twice before I do a thing, if I possibly can, though I have just read a very funny anecdote about that very saying."

"What was it?" said his father.

"It was this: An old gentleman had a black servant, who always acted as if he had no head, or might as well have been without one—something like me, I suppose; but his master tried his best to put some sense into his head, and did not omit to tell him, at least fifty times a day, 'Now, Cato, always think twice, before you speak once,' until at last Cato got it by heart. One evening the poor old gentleman fell fast asleep, while he was reading the newspaper. He held in his hand a lighted candle. All at once his head went bob, bob, right into the candle, and instantly his wig took fire! Cato came in at this very instant. Here was a chance! Now he could win his master's approval, by putting the oft-repeated adage into practice, so he cried aloud, 'Massa, I tink once—Massa, I tink twice—Massa, your wig on fire!' and then rushed to his master, who was now wide awake, his wig blazing like a chimney, and tore it off, though not before the poor old gentleman had received a pretty severe scorching. Now what do you think of that, papa?" continued Charlie, looking very mischievous.

His father laughed, and answered: "That was a very unfortunate application of very good advice, but another old saying is, "There are exceptions to every rule," and, in some cases you must act on the instant to do any good; but, with these exceptions, prudence, reflection and, above all, a careful regard to the whisperings of conscience, and a constant appeal to your Father in heaven, to guide your steps aright, will go far towards making you the good boy, and good man, I hope and pray you will become; do try, my dear son, to overcome this dangerous fault in your character."

Charlie looked very grave, and made a great many resolutions to be a perfect pattern of prudence from that time forth, but, alas! these good resolutions must have flown to the moon, for he kept them but a very short time, as (with great sorrow) I shall tell you.

The heedless boy was very fond of reading, and, as you may suppose, the books he liked the most were "Robinson Crusoe," "Gulliver's Travels," and "Peter Wilkins," because they were so full of adventures.

He was so excited by Robinson Crusoe, that if he had dared, he would have gone off to sea to look for a desolate island, and be Robinson Crusoe number two; but he was a little too much in awe of his father for that, and he might never have had an adventure if he had not chanced one morning upon a party of gipsies sitting around a fire in a wood, near his home. Their glittering eyes, swarthy complexions, and air of careless enjoyment, fired the boy's imagination. It gave him a new idea. Splendid! The very thing! What perfect happiness! The woods were large, and he could run off and be a gipsy immediately. It was as plain as A B C that he would have a first-rate time.

It was school vacation just then—lovely summer weather. The white clouds, which the sweet south wind wafted along, deepened by contrast the glorious blue heaven above; the sweet, tranquil, drowsy country sounds; the grassy, daisy-spangled banks of the noisy little brook; and the great dark, thick woods, so rich in foliage that the sun's rays made only dimples beneath, that came and went as the leaves were stirred. All these beautiful things made a life in the joyous, free, open air, seem the very embodiment of happiness, and Charlie, without a thought of the consequences, determined to be a gipsy without a moment's loss of time.

It happened—by good chance or by bad chance—that, at this very moment,

Arthur, Harry, Richard and George, (Harry's little brother,) friends and schoolmates of Charlie's, came to ask him to go fishing with them. What an opportunity! Five jolly fellows together! As they went along he would invite them to be his band, and he would be the captain. Capital!

The boys shouldered their fishing rods, and started off, now darting after a butterfly, now jumping over a boulder, as boys always do; every one in the highest spirits, and quite ready for the first fun that offered.

They soon arrived at the water, and, in a very short time, had caught a dozen fish, when Charlie, with sparkling eyes, began—

"I say, fellows, I am going to turn gipsy. Don't you want to go along?"

"What for?" drawled Arthur, who was rather a slow coach.

"What for? why, for fun. Who wants to be shut up at home all the time, and have an old granny of a nurse blowing him up because his hands are dirty, or because he don't come home, before the dinner bell rings, to have his hair brushed and his jacket twitched straight. Now, out in the woods we can be as dirty as we please, and nobody can say boo! and the dinners will come to us, and we won't have to run the moment a bell rings."

"But suppose the dinners don't come?" suggested Richard, who was very fond of pastry and cakes, "I, for one, can't live on stewed moonshine and mustard. If that is to be served up, I shall wish I was out of the woods, and home again."

"I'll go with you," shouted Harry.

"And I," said little George, imitating his brother. "Come along, we are all ready; the longer we stand, the *fearder* we'll be. Hurra! hurra!"

"That's you! all right!" cried Charlie, joyfully. "I tell you, I've every thing fixed,—that is, in my *head*. Hurra! for a gipsy life, and a camp in the wild woods free, with a kettle hung up on sticks, and all sorts of goodies for tea. There's some poetry for you!"

And now, laughing, and excited by their anticipations, off they all started, dragging their fish along, and stumbling through the bushes, to get clear of the wood paths, and bury themselves in the thickest part of the forest. It was a long time before they found a place that seemed lonely enough, but they did discover just the right place at last—a small, open spot, sweet enough and secluded enough to have made a ball-room for the fairies; and Charlie's handsome eyes fairly danced with delight, as he threw himself down, and cried:

"Here we are, boys! splendid place this! Trees all around, and the ground carpeted with beautiful soft moss."

"All but the soft," growled Richard, jumping up, and making a variety of wry faces. "Only look what a great thorn I have sat down upon. I'm half killed. I wonder what thorns were made for?"

"For four-legged gentlemen, with very long ears," answered Arthur. "They are perfectly devoted to them. I think it's very odd you should be so fond of thorns, as you are not a donkey."

"Fond—fiddlesticks! Let a fellow alone, can't you?"

"Don't tease him, Arthur," cried Charlie. "Here, I say, all of you, guess this: Mr. Martingale has ten fine horses, and there are only twenty-four feet among them all."

"Twenty four feet!" said Harry; "impossible! You say they are fine horses, and ten of them. Every horse has four feet, and four times ten are forty— that's certain."

"Perhaps," said little George, "some of them are a new style of horse; six have the right number of feet, making the twenty-four, and the rest crawl on their bellies, like snakes."

"Goodness! how absurd!" exclaimed Arthur. "I have heard of Mr. Barnum's woolly horse, and a saw-horse, and a chestnut horse, and a horse-chestnut; and a flying-horse, and a horse-fly; and a clothes-horse, and a horse-cloth; and a rocking-horse. But a snake-horse is something new."

"Give it up?" said Charlie. "Suppose you alter the spelling a little."

"Oh! I have it!" shouted Arthur. "The horses had twenty *fore* feet, and they also had twenty *hind* feet. That's the best catch I ever heard. Just see, fellows, what comes of being head-boy in spelling-class. I'm the boy for learning! I dare say Dr. Addup is crying his eyes out, because it is vacation, and he won't see me for a month."

"I've got twenty-four appetites," said Richard; "when is the plum-pudding coming up?"

"The fish for the first course, and here they are," said Charlie.

"But I don't like raw fish," said George; "and where is the fire to cook 'em?"

"Don't be in a hurry," said the captain. "I'll fix that in a minute; I know all about it—read it in a book; all you have to do, is, to find two sticks, and rub them together, and there's your fire right off."

But our young gipsy soon found the difference between a fire with two

14

sticks in a book, and a fire with two sticks in a wood. He rubbed his two sticks together, until *he* was in a perfect blaze with the exertion, but the blaze he wanted would not come.

"Hang the sticks!" he exclaimed; "the people in the books always did it so easily, why can't I?"

Luckily for the success of the gipsy party, one of the band just then happened to spy a match, which some chance wanderer had dropped, and a few dry sticks having been hastily collected, a fine fire was soon crackling and snapping merrily.

Delighted with their success, they next held a grand consultation, on the noble science of cooking.

"The gipsies hang a kettle on forked sticks," said Richard; "and fish, flesh, and fowl are all put in together, making, what I should call, stewed hodge-podge."

"Well, there are ninety-nine reasons why we won't use the kettle," said Arthur, who considered himself the wit of the party,—"and the first is, we have no kettle, so I won't trouble you with the rest. Good gracious!" he continued, "I'm so hungry, I could eat what I perfectly hate, and that's a boiled calf's head."

"And I forty sour apples," cried Harry. "I wish one of these trees could be turned into hot ginger-bread, wouldn't we *pitch in?*"

As there was no kettle to be had, they endeavored to fry the fish by sticking them on the top of forked sticks. But, somehow, the fish would not stay "stuck." They fell off into the blaze, and smoked, and "sizzled," and smelt like any thing but delicious food; and there was great scorching of fingers, and singeing of hair, as the new cooks tried to twitch them out. At last, covered with ashes, and, of course, without plates or any other civilized comfort, the banquet was "served" in the young gentlemen's fingers, and tea began, Richard declaring he was "hungry enough to eat a rhinoceros."

The first mouthful tasted "first rate," but, presently Arthur sang out, "Hollo! I'm choking! my mouth's full of scales, and there is something inside of this fish, that I never saw at home."

"Oh, goodness! I never thought of cleaning them; how stupid!" said Charlie; "Never mind, boys! we'll know better next time."

"But I want some salt, and some bread and butter," said little George; "Robinson Crusoe had them."

"Where's my ship, to get all these things," said Charlie; "we're not on an island."

"But I thought you said you had every thing fixed."

"So I did—in my head; but you see—" answered Charlie, hesitating and scratching his head, and looking very much bothered—"you see—"

"Come, come, boys," interposed Harry, "no fighting in the camp; we are a sort of greenhorn gipsies, now, but we shall be all right by-and-bye, and have a first-rate time. I wish I had a drink of water—but never mind. Hurrah for the gipsies, and success to our side!"

Harry's good humor infected the rest of the party, and their hunger being quieted by the meal, bad as it was, they piled more sticks on the fire, just for the pleasure of seeing them burn, and sat down at a little distance, to tell stories to each other, of all the gipsies, and wild adventures they could remember.

By this time the glorious flush of sunset rested upon every thing. The little fairy glade, with the fire in its centre; the handsome, animated faces of the thoughtless boys, as they sat grouped together in careless but not ungraceful attitudes; the crimson, purple, and golden clouds above, altogether, made a very charming picture, and, so far, gipsy life certainly seemed *coleur de rose*.

But the shadows gradually lengthened; the glowing colors became fainter; and the gray twilight came stealing on. Occasionally a dissipated little bird would give a faint twitter, as he was hurrying home in the deepening gloom, from a late dinner party. Insensibly the boys relapsed into silence, and, wearied with their long tramp, began to think of going to bed; but here commenced new troubles.

"The beds! and the tents! Even the real gipsies did not sleep upon the bare ground—what was to be done?"

"Here's a pretty how-de-do!" cried Arthur; "this is worse than the fish and the fire; matches may be sometimes dropped in the woods, but mattresses never," and here poor Charlie came in for a scolding chorus from every body.

"Let's get some big branches, and lean them against a tree," said little George.

"Where's the axe to cut them with," said Richard.

"Dig a cave," cried Harry.

"What with—our nails? I have a jackknife," said Richard, "I'll lend it to you; suppose *you* begin."

Charlie's face looked about as blank as this O, while the boys were talking.

He was completely nonplussed, and too proud to acknowledge it. And now, for the first time, his father's warning voice rose in his memory, and in the midst of his vexation, another voice, "the still small voice" of conscience, reproached him for having acted with silly impetuosity; and this time he had brought his friends, as well as himself, into discomfort and trouble. A bitter repentant tear came into his eye, but he hastily dashed it away, with the cuff of his sleeve. By this time all was dark; there was no moon that night, and the stars, blinking and twinkling in their far-off homes, gave scarcely a glimmer of light in the dense forest. The burning twigs alone revealed to Charlie the wearied, vexed faces of his companions. Throwing his hair back from his forehead, by the quick, characteristic movement I have mentioned, he said cheerfully:

"I tell you what, fellows, we are here, and we must stay here to-night, at least. We can't burrow like rabbits, and we don't understand roosting on one foot like birds; suppose we all lie down in a heap, one top of the other, and, when the bottom one of all is warm enough, take him out and put him on top."

This made the boys roar with laughter, and at last, somehow or other, they squeezed, and pushed, and tumbled, and jumbled themselves together, like a family of kittens, and not a soul could tell which were his own arms or legs, as they stuck out, over, under, and across each other, and then they shut their eyes, and tried to fall asleep.

But here new troubles began. Myriads of insects came buzzing around them, a superannuated old bull-frog and his wife set up a dismal bellowing, in a swampy spot close by, and, apparently, any quantity of high-tempered owls were holding a mass meeting, all hooting and tooting, and talking at once. A general attack was made on the poor little gipsies by a nimble army of musquitoes, who seemed to be in a perfect frenzy of delight, at the fine supper provided for them. The boys slapped, and whacked, and kicked in the dark, and hit each other, three times as often as they did their foes.

"Oh, murderation!" exclaimed poor Charlie, "what shall we do—what *shall* we do?" as the boys, unable to bear the torment any longer, started to their feet, little George fairly blubbering with distress, and rummaging in vain in his pocket, for his pocket-handkerchief, to wipe away his tears, and rub his nose up, as little boys invariably do.

"Suppose we try to find some other place," said Richard, "we seem to have come to the very spot where all the musquitoes live."

"Oh! don't," cried little George, "don't go running about the woods in the dark. Who knows how many bears there may be up in the trees."

"And robbers, too, with guns and pistols," said Arthur.

"And how can we light another fire, if we leave this?" said Richard, who was more practical than the rest. "By-the-way, I think I've heard that smoke will drive away musquitoes; suppose we put on some green wood, and make a great smudge."

Any thing was better than being bitten; so the boys poked and groped around in the uncertain light, for the fire was very low, and picked up all the branches they could find, and heaped them upon the fire, and, sure enough, they did make a great "smudge," and set every body coughing, choking, and crying, until they were half crazy.

By degrees the musquitoes did seem to be driven off a little, or else the gipsies were so tired and sleepy that they ceased to hear or feel them, for one after another became, first silent, then drowsy, and, finally, dropped off into slumber, too sound to be easily broken.

It was now midnight. The weary faces of these thoughtless, naughty boys were now and then revealed by a fitful gleam of the dying fire; the leaves of the trees were motionless; and there was a sudden hush and stillness in the air, as if nature, too, was weary, and had sunk into a deathlike sleep. Presently faint mutterings were heard; the stars disappeared, and the darkness became intense; great masses of black clouds rolled up to the zenith, and came swiftly down on the other side; the air freshened, and, in a moment, the tops of the giant trees bent their proud heads, and a rustling, rushing, crashing sound came through their branches as the wind swept by, in its fury breaking off small twigs with a crackling noise, and hurling them with innumerable leaves to the ground.

Suddenly a fierce, sharp flash of lightning leaped from the clouds, instantly succeeded by a tremendous, rattling clap of thunder awakening the boys, who, with screams of horror, started to their feet and clung to each other in terror.

For an instant after there was a dead, solemn silence, and then came the first great drops of rain pattering through the leaves, and again the trees were tossed by the blast like the angry waves of a stormy sea.

And now the rain descended in torrents, forked lightning blinded the eyes, and the crashing thunder was deafening. Heart-stricken, and wild with terror, the unhappy gipsies clung together, the rain drenching them to the skin; and poor little George, dizzy with fright, reeled and fell to the ground, and the boys, in their agony, thought he was dead.

Charley, broken-hearted, fell on his knees and, with tears streaming down his face, implored God to forgive him, and bring George back to life, and not inflict upon him this awful—awful punishment. He felt like a murderer. *He* alone was to blame; *he* had been the tempter, and his father had truly said that there were two things that followed the yielding to temptation—sin and repentance. He did repent. If he could only get back home with his dear companions, he would—he *would* be a steady boy ever after.

With trembling hands he lifted up little George's head, and entreated him to speak one word to him—"only one single word." A low groan, and a faint "Oh, Harry, take me home!" issued from the childish lips, to Charley's great joy; and his brother and the rest hung round, trying to keep the rain off, and saying, "Don't give up, little fellow! try to bear it a little longer; the storm is almost over."

Hark! what was that they heard? A far-off, distant shout. They listened with painful intentness. It came faintly again: "Hol-lo!" It must be—it was—yes—somebody was calling them; and, altogether, they gave a shrill cry of joy! Their hearts beat wildly. The shouts sounded louder. They hear their names called: Char-ley—Har-ry! They answer again, trembling—their whole frames thrilling. Lights come dancing through the trees at a distance. They are coming nearer; and the boys, taking George in their arms, struggle through the wet branches with which the wind has covered the ground. In another moment they can dimly discern two men carrying lanterns, and Charley recognizes his father's voice.

"Here they are! they are found! they are safe!" and Charley, gasping for breath, leaps into his father's arms. He feels the hot tears on his cheek, and hears the broken voice say, "Oh, my son—my son! Thank God, I have found you at last." Not one word of reproach; but those dreadful tears—his father crying, and for him. He felt to his very heart's core what a wicked, ungrateful boy he had been.

With many sobs and broken words, he implored forgiveness. If his dear father would only love him as he did before, he would never—never grieve him again.

Harry's father embraced his lost boys with thankful joy; and both parents shook hands, and spoke kindly to Arthur and Richard. No word of reproach was uttered; and George, excited by his beloved father's voice, rallied, and seemed for the time almost well again.

The forest was very extensive, and the woods presented so little variety that you might go round and round in a circuit for days, thinking you were taking the most direct path out. If the little gipsies had not been thus found, through the guidance of a divine Providence, they might, and very probably would, have starved to death before assistance came to them.

19

And now the day begins to dawn. Rosy streaks shoot up into the zenith; and the birds sing with a rollicking gladness, as if they rejoiced over the rescue of the weary little band of gipsies—soon to be gipsies no longer. And, truly, they presented a most dismal and bedraggled appearance, with their hair full of broken bits of dried leaves, their faces streaked and disfigured with traces of tears, and their clothes soiled and wet. Wearily they toiled through the broken and tangled branches that lay upon the ground, and little George very soon had to be lifted tenderly into his father's arms. His face grew flushed and his voice hoarse, as he murmured, "Oh, papa, my throat hurts me so!" and his father saw with anguish that his little boy was very ill, and they were yet, as well as he could judge, some miles from home.

But how can I depict the sufferings of the poor mothers, who were left at home mourning, watching, and waiting, and becoming paler and more hopeless as the night slowly and painfully wore on!

The gray light of morning broke through the crevices of the closed shutters of those desolated homes, but it made them seem only the darker, for "*they*" had not come. And it was nearly two hours after sunrise before an unusual stir and bustle outside sent the blood in quick tides through the frames of these poor mothers. Suddenly they hear a joyful shout! they rush to the windows; they see their children coming. And now—only *now*, does the day brighten for them.

I have no words to describe the meeting. I am sure the boys will never forget the pale, tear-stained faces, which told of so much anguish suffered for them, or the trembling kisses they received, while a prayer of thankfulness ascended to heaven that the lost ones were found. Still, not a word of reproach. With a mixture of remorse and happiness, they hastened to remove all vestige of their gipsy life, and, with clean faces and hands, and thankful hearts, sat down to a nicely served and most welcome breakfast.

All but poor little George. He was ill for a long, long time, and Charlie shed many a bitter tear of self-reproach while his life was in danger; and, when he began to get better, the repentant boy was unwearied in coming to read pleasant stories to him, and to bring him every nice toy of his own, and beg his mother for little delicacies to tempt his sickly appetite.

In a few days, when Charlie had somewhat recovered his cheerfulness, his father had a kind, friendly talk with him in his library, (see picture); he pointed out to his son the folly and danger of yielding to every impulse, without first finding out whether it would lead to good results. Charlie listened to all his father said with respectful attention, and, I am sure, he profited by his excellent advice, for all this that I am telling you happened some years ago, and though I know Charlie intimately, and believe that it is impossible to do right all at once, still his past sad experience has had a wonderful effect, and when he feels tempted, by a hasty impulse, to do any thing particularly head-over-heels, he is sure to be arrested in time, by a still small voice within, which whispers, REMEMBER WHAT CAME OF GIPSYING.

Charlie's Father talking to him.

THE CHILD HEROINE.

On a clear balmy morning in July, six years ago, two magnificent steamboats, the Henry Clay and the America, left Albany at the same time, for New York. A gentle breeze just curled the waters of the noble and beautiful Hudson River. Both boats were filled with happy-looking people, and the bustle of departure, the laughing voices, and general hilarity, combined with the bright, blue sky above, contributed to raise the spirits, and fill every one with that exhilarating gladness, which makes the mere physical sense of living and breathing a happiness.

And now the rush and roar of steam arose; the ponderous wheels make great waves in the hitherto tranquil tide, and, with the cry of "All aboard," the stately boats cleave their paths through the waters, and move swiftly down the river.

Too swiftly, for they were racing, and on the Henry Clay, especially, the captain and officers, excited and reckless, were crowding on steam, and forcing the boat to her utmost speed. For a while some of the passengers enjoyed the race, and urged and encouraged the officers to "go ahead," and one comfortable, fat old lady, who was going down to "York market, with farm produce, consisting of fat pork, butter, and various kinds of *sass*," and who was certainly old enough and ugly enough to know better, was in such a high state of exhilaration at the bustle and fun of the race, that she could not keep still an instant. She answered every body's questions she chanced to hear, whether addressed to her or not, and when the Henry Clay fell back a very little the foolish old soul twitched off her spectacles, set her arms a-kimbo, and declared "she never seed sich a goosey gander of a capting," and straightway fell into such a state of worry and excitement, that a waggish young gentleman, standing near, solemnly advised her to do like another silly old lady, under similar circumstances, who hobbled up to the captain and screamed in his ears, "Capting, now don't you give it up now; now, don't now; ef all your wood is out, capting, I've got a bar'l of fat pork aboard— could you put that on the fire to help on the steam?"

Swiftly the boats sped past the smiling, picturesque villages dotting each side, and entered the bolder parts of the majestic river, where the high banks curve sharply round into mimic bays. And now the passengers, seeing the great danger in these sudden turns, vainly entreated the captain of the Henry Clay to give up the race, and have a regard for their lives. But his passions were aroused, and he turned a deaf ear to their remonstrances; he cared nothing for their precious lives in comparison with being beaten by his opponent; and he was only awakened to a sense of his broken trust, by a shriek of horror and a simultaneous crash! as the America came into violent collision with the Henry Clay.

Fortunately the damage done was not great; but the people on the Henry Clay had not recovered from their fright and excitement, as she stopped at Poughkeepsie to receive more passengers.

Waiting at the wharf was a tall, fair and graceful lady. She held by the hand a sweet little girl, about ten years of age, whose large, dark, dreamy eyes, transparent purity of complexion, and great delicacy of form and feature, caused her to seem scarcely an inhabitant of earth, but rather an ærial being, whom a breath of wind might melt away like a summer cloud. Not that the little one was either sad or grave; on the contrary, as she held her mother's hand a continual little dancing motion, and a childish song, that came in broken snatches from her rosy and beautiful mouth, caused many to turn and smile upon her, and rejoice in her innocent gayety.

"Now, dear mother," said Maggie, in a sweet coaxing voice, "let us hurry on board, or the boat will leave us. I want to see my dear father this very night."

But the mother had a vague presentiment that made her reluctant to go. She observed the excitement, and apparent confusion, on the crowded boat, and if she had not thought that yielding to a presentiment was foolish, she would have turned back. As it was, after hesitating until the last moment, she stepped on board, trembling at she knew not what, and her feelings of disquiet were greatly increased, when the ladies in the saloon informed her of the disaster that had already occurred.

But little Maggie, in her childlike and happy ignorance of any thing to fear, was delighted with all she saw. She flitted hither and thither, with her little dancing step, and her bird-like song, now gazing at the diamond sparkles in the river, now peering fearfully down into the raging depths of the great iron monster who, with seething sighs and hoarse groans, was bearing them along.

Many were the smiles and blessings that followed the dainty little lady as she glided about, and if any sought to detain her she answered their questions with a kind of child-like dignity, mingled with bashfulness enchanting to behold, and then darted back to her mother, whose melancholy eyes were

24

always on the watch.

What is that they hear? A cry of "fire! fire! The boat is on fire!"

Maggie on board the Steamer.

With a thrill of horror every person in the saloon arose and rushed to the doors, and Maggie, with a shrill scream of terror, fell into her mother's arms. The ladies were rudely pushed back by the men in charge of the boat, with an assurance that there was "no danger," and they must "keep quiet," and the doors were shut upon them. They heard the frantic cries outside, and a dense smoke came in upon them. Bewildered, despairing, fainting on every side, a scene of indescribable distress and confusion ensued. The flames were approaching. Already they felt their scorching breath, and the distracted mother, with a burst of passionate tears, folded her child, her sweet Margaret, her "pearl"—so truly named—in her arms, and prepared for death.

Choked with her sobs, but struggling to speak calmly, she said, "My darling

25

child—my own little Maggie,—life is sweet to both of us: *but we must die!* The awful flames are coming nearer every moment. I cannot bear to think, that my darling should die by the torture of fire. Let us bid each other good-bye, Maggie, and jump into the water. We shall not suffer long; but, oh! how bitter to think I shall never more look upon my husband's face—never embrace my two noble boys!"

With a wild, despairing cry issuing from her white, parted lips, Maggie clung to her mother, and sobbed out, "Oh, mother! I cannot jump—I cannot jump! I am afraid!" and her sweet little face grew more ghastly with terror. "Some one will surely come, dear mother; they will not let us die without trying to save us. Oh! they will *try* to come! They will not let a poor little girl burn up in these dreadful flames! and if they save me, *I will save you, mother! I will never go without you!*"

But, alas! all was in the wildest, the most frantic confusion. The panic-stricken passengers, pressing upon each other, were jumping and falling overboard in every direction. The fire separated the two extremes of the boat, and no help or succor was near. And now came the pang of parting. For a brief, agonizing moment, the mother held her child in her arms, then drew her to one of the windows.

All at once, a wonderful change came over the little tender child. For one moment, a radiant flush lighted up the sweet face, and then died away, leaving a deathly paleness as before, but with it a rapt, angelic expression, as if, in that moment, a loving, merciful Father had given the pure spirit a glimpse of heaven.

Drawing her garments closely about her, she said, "Kiss me, dear mother, I am going;" and, climbing through the window, she leapt into the water—in her eyes the same uplifted, celestial expression, as she sank beneath the wave. God, in His mercy, had taken away the sting of death. Little Maggie was going HOME.

The poor mother turned away in agony; then, with a prayer that their sufferings might be short, she followed her child, and the waves closed over her.

But now the ways of God, which are not our ways, became manifest. Maggie's buoyant form rose out of the water directly under one of the stanchions, which supported that part of the deck projecting beyond the hull. Gasping, panting, and almost senseless, she instinctively clutched at this, and passing her arm around it, hung there, half in, half out of the water. As she regained her consciousness, she looked vainly around for her mother, and the poor little child became convulsed with terror, at finding herself alone in this painful and fearful position.

At this moment, Maggie felt something coming to the surface directly beneath her, and to her joy, recognized her mother's bonnet. Grasping it with all her little strength, what was her horror to feel it give way, and remain in her hand, while her mother sank slowly down again out of sight! Coming up the second time, the child, with desperate energy, clutched at her hair, and this time raised her mother's head above the water.

"Mother, mother!" she cried, "here I am—your own little Maggie. Speak to me, oh! speak to me, mother, or I shall die!"

The large hazel eyes of the mother unclosed, and, struggling with the water that was choking her, she murmured,—"Thank God! thank God! we may yet be saved."

"Oh, yes, mother," answered the little one, "God did not mean that we should die. I will hold you up, until my arm burns off. Don't be afraid—I will never let you go. Only see, dear mother, how strong I am. I have wound your long hair all round my hand. Do not shut your eyes, dear mother—look at me. While you look at me, I can bear any thing."

And now, the cruel, hungry flames were bursting through the hull, and the poor, little strained arm that supported them both, was scorching, and the hand was *burning*! but the brave heart of the child flinched not; earthly pain had no power over her; an *overshadowing presence* sustained the little spirit. *She even smiled*—that brave child!—that her mother should not know the fierce pain she was enduring. But at last, her strength began to fail; an intense ashen paleness overspread her lovely face, and the large, soul-lit eyes were now bent upon the shore with a look so piteous—so appealing! Oh! how long it seemed! Would help never—*never* come?

A few moments more, and it would be too late. But now they are seen by a gentleman on shore. He rushes to a boat lying at the dock, and offers the owner a reward if he will row him to the drowning lady and child.

"I can't go," said the man. "It is too dangerous. I am waiting to see the boiler burst. I expect it to burst every moment."

"Will you suffer those poor unfortunates to perish before our eyes, you heartless fellow?" remonstrated the other. "Give me the oars—I will go alone."

"I will not," growled the man. "It is no use. You can't save them, and you will lose your own life. I tell you, the boiler will burst, and you will be killed."

But with one effort of his powerful arm, this good Samaritan hurled the boatman away, and jumping into the boat, and springing to the oars, he soon rowed to where little Maggie hung, her arm, by this time, wrenched, strained, and burned, beyond the endurance of many a strong man.

Supporting the mother with one arm, with the other, he tenderly lifted the poor little sufferer into the boat. Her mother was so much exhausted, that it was with the utmost difficulty he raised her out of the water; and, although he rowed quickly back, she was perfectly senseless when she was laid on the beach.

And now, Maggie watched with alarm and anxiety the means used to bring her mother back to life.

After a while they were successful, and then, with such dry clothes as could be hastily procured, the grateful pair departed, on the Hudson River Railroad for New York, accompanied by the gentleman who had so generously risked his life to save theirs.

In the rail-car, Maggie's mother fainted. Her strength was utterly gone, from long exposure to the water. With earnest sympathy, the kind-hearted gentleman once more came to their relief. He took off his coat and wrapped it around her, and the increased warmth it afforded soon restored her to consciousness. A dim recollection crossed her mind, as she looked up to thank their "friend in need." Another look, and she recognized, to her great surprise and pleasure, one whom she had known well many years ago; and he was doubly thankful that he had been an instrument, in the hands of God, of saving from a violent death a lady for whom, through long years of separation, he had retained the highest esteem and friendship.

And now, dear little reader, I must tell you, the wonderful telegraph had sent the news of the burning of the steamboat to New York, while yet the panic-stricken passengers were making their awful choice of death by fire or water, and little Maggie's father was one of the first at the terrible scene. He knew that his wife and daughter were to return in this boat, and with anguish he searched upon the beach, and looked into the faces of the dead, dreading to find his loved ones among them.

But they were not there. Then he went down to the water side, and, nearly all that dreadful night, he dived to the bottom again and again, bringing up many a poor victim, and every time his cheek grew paler and his heart throbbed more wildly. At last, exhausted and despairing, he gave up the dreadful task. They were gone for ever—he should never again see even the dead faces of his dear wife and his sweet little "pearl of great price."

Suddenly a faint hope, like a far-off star, dawned upon his heart. It was just possible that Maggie and her mother were safe in Poughkeepsie; they might have changed their minds at the last moment. An engine was there ready to start; it was offered to him. He gratefully accepted, and, without a single car, the engineer and himself jumped upon the panting iron monster and almost flew back to Poughkeepsie.

Alas! *they had gone*. These terrible words blanched his cheek again, and, all hope deserting him—utterly broken down, the strong man covered his face with his hands and burst into a passionate flood of tears. His wife—his dear companion, and his little Margaret—his tender, delicate bud of promise, to be burned—burned, till nothing human was left of them, or else now lying among the rocks beneath the waters. It was too horrible. It must not be. He would go back; he would try once more. Surely, this time, he would recover the drowned bodies of those he loved so well; and then, at least, he would have the melancholy comfort of knowing that they were tenderly and reverently laid in the earth.

In the gray dawn of the morning he came back to Yonkers, where the remains of the still burning steamer lay, and hastened once more to the beach. Preparing once more to dive into the river again, a simple object—a child's bonnet met his eye, floating on the water. *It was Maggie's bonnet*. His heart stood still; his blood froze in his veins; his eyes strained wildly after the little token of his dreadful loss, as it floated idly by, its wet and stained blue ribbons fluttering in the summer breeze. He neither spoke nor stirred; he seemed turned into stone; his hands clasped tightly together, and his gaze fastened upon that tiny, but terrible sign of the hapless fate of his wife and child. The pitying bystanders tried to arouse and draw him away. They assured him that it was useless to attempt finding any more bodies—every possible effort had been made; and, at length, the heart-broken man went sadly away to return to his desolated home.

When he arrived in the street where he lived, and drew near the familiar house, a shudder came over him. Little Maggie had always watched for him at the door, to spring into his arms and receive "the first kiss." With a keen pang at his heart and a smothered groan, he murmured, "They are gone—they are *dead*. Oh, I cannot go there! I shall be mad if I do."

But suddenly One stood by his side invisible to mortal eyes, and there came into his heart, like a soft, sweet strain of heavenly music, these words, "Blessed are they that mourn, for they shall be comforted."

Great tears came to his relief, and softened the fierce pain at his heart; and now, with deep-drawn sighs, he entered first a neighbor's house to seek that sympathy which his sorely stricken soul had before refused, and which would give him strength to enter the home where *they* were *not*.

His friends met him with extended hands and glad voices, exclaiming, "Oh, how glad we are that you have come! We rejoice with you that your dear ones are safe."

"Safe—SAFE?" he cried, "do you mock me in my misery?"

"Why," they answered, "do you not know that they have returned, and are safe in your house?"

With a cry that rent the air, Maggie's father rushed out of the door and into his own house, and in a moment his wife and his dear little child were clasped tight in his arms—his shrieks of hysterical laughter, mingled with the great sobs that convulsed his frame, showing, too plainly, alas! that joy had finished what grief began; for now he had indeed lost his senses. The sudden revulsion had been too much; but, after a while, the gentle soothings of his wife and the loving caresses of Maggie restored him to himself; and soon he was ready to listen to the wonderful account of their escape—many times interrupting the narrative to fold his little Maggie, with tears, to his breast, and to thank God again and again for the blessing of such a child.

And now, dear little reader, Maggie has grown up to be a young lady. She has the same dark, thoughtful eyes and transparent purity of complexion. She flits about her father's house like a sunbeam, bringing joy and delight into his heart, and her voice issues from her beautiful mouth so sweet and clear that it seems like the singing of a lark. With the thrilling memory of the past ever before him, her father oftentimes gazes into her sweet young face with an earnest tenderness impossible to describe.

I wish every girl and boy that will read this could have known Maggie when she was a child; they would have wondered how such a delicate little creature could have shown so much courage and endurance. It seems incredible, and yet every word I have written is true.

I also wish that I could tell them her whole name; but I promised, when permission was given me to write this account of heroism, I would not tell her name, or even where she lived. But I *will* tell this much: She lives, at this very moment, on a beautiful island, very near the city of New York; and she is so modest and retiring that her very next-door neighbor does not suspect he is living close to THE CHILD HEROINE!

AUNT MARY.

A SKETCH BY A GIRL OF FIFTEEN.

IT is my opinion, that in spite of my being quite a simple young girl, I might, without exciting much surprise, personate the character of a respectable old lady; for all kinds of antiquities seem to agree extremely well with me.

Thus, an old book has a peculiar charm for me; an old dress always sets better than a new one; and, certainly, every one will allow, that there is no comfort in the world equal to a pair of old slippers.

But most particularly am I fond of old ladies and gentlemen, with their quaint stories of the days when they were young; those magical days, when the sun shone quite differently from now—"so much longer and brighter;" the soft summer breezes were sweeter and cooler, and the winter snows were not the six-inch-deep affairs, we have at present, but were up to the second-story windows; then the birds sang far more sweetly than they ever do now-a-days: the peaches were twice as large, the apples three times, and the gentlemen bowed four times lower, and twenty times more respectfully.

The dearest of all my elderly relatives, is my mother's aunt—my Great-aunt Mary. I wish you could see her sitting in a corner of the fireplace, in a funny little black rocking-chair of hers, that is, no one knows how old, with a mosaic patch-work cover on the back, always busy with her knitting or sewing, and just the dearest, sweetest little old soul in the world; though she is my *great* aunt, I am so much larger and stronger, that I could, if I pleased, catch her up in my arms, and run all over the house with her, without her being able to help herself. I mean to try it, sometime.

Aunt Mary's face is wrinkled, but her blue eyes are still clear and bright— her soft gray hair is parted over a placid brow, her smile is very sweet, and her voice so pleasant and kindly, that you feel as though you could never do enough for her, and you love her instinctively, the very first time you see her. I believe that is the reason everybody calls her "Aunt Mary;" it seems as if they could not help it, but I think it a great liberty.

Aunt Mary is not one of those *old* old ladies, who think little folks should sit upright on a hard wooden bench, with nothing to rest their poor little tired spines against, and nothing to do but stare at the fire, and twirl their thumbs.

She took a great-nephew of hers to church, not long ago, a little bit of a fellow, and, I think, a perfect darling. Stanny had never been to church before, and he was so surprised with the great painted windows, and the quantity of people, that he sat up, in wondering silence, as grave as a judge; and Aunt Mary was just thinking, to herself, "How well Stanny behaves! really, I am quite proud of him,"—when, suddenly, the organ struck up very loud, and Stanny, well remembering the organs in the street, which he always ran to the window to see, shouted out loud: "Why, Aunt Mary! there is an organ! but where is the monkey?" Of course, everybody round laughed; how could they help it? and dear old Aunt Mary, instead of wanting to shake his head off—as some old ladies would—laughed, too, but whispered to him to speak more softly next time, and gave him a gum-drop out of her pocket.

She loves all the children, and is the soul of indulgence to all her little nephews and nieces, and don't scold a bit when they run away with her snuff-box, as Fanny and I have often done; although she is naturally very quick-tempered, her patience and forbearance are beautiful to observe.

Aunt Mary never uses spectacles; she reads the finest print, and stitches far more neatly than I can, without them; and those faded but small and pretty hands, have knit more stockings for the poor, and made more patch-work bed-quilts, than I have time to count.

Then she is very lively, and has often made me shout with laughter; her comical expressions, with many a quiet sly cut at our faults and nonsensical notions, and her funny stories, are far better than the writings of many an author, who tries to write as though his fun was not the hardest work in the world for him, instead of coming right from his heart, like my dear Aunt Mary's. Time has not soured her, as it does some old people; you never see her going about, with her brows tied up in—oh! such a hard knot—with a querulous moan of: "W-h-e-r-e-'s my spectacles? why d-o-n-'t you come and light my fire? who's got my snuff-box? oh, dear!" Not at all! but it is: "Do let me read you this in the paper"—a noble act of heroism, or a funny anecdote, that has excited her admiration, or laughter; and, presently, we will all be admiring, or laughing with her, to her immense satisfaction.

You can't get Aunt Mary to put on a hoop petticoat, or wear gaiter boots. She remains steadfastly by her narrow skirts and prunella shoes.

Once, as a very great favor, she permitted me to try on a dress of hers, which she wore to her first ball, when she was about sixteen years old. You may imagine what a singular figure I made in it, when I tell you that there were but two breadths in the skirt, and tiny gores at the side; while the sleeves stood out, as though they were lined with buckram, and the waistband came just under my arms. The material was the thickest of white silk, with lovely bunches of roses all over it. You perceive that fashions have changed considerably since she was a girl; and, I often think, how queer it must seem, for her to look back on all the fashions that have come up since her first ball dress.

And now, I will tell you something very interesting, indeed, about Aunt Mary. She has seen the great General Washington, alive; and I would be willing to be just as old, if I could say the same.

Yes, my dear old aunt is of another and past century. It always seems to me, as though she should be dressed with the powder, high-heeled shoes, and ruffles of real lace that she wore long ago.

But in any dress we shall always love her dearly; for she is to us a kind monitor, a sincere friend, and a simple, earnest Christian. God bless dear Aunt Mary.

LITTLE PETER.

OF all the funny little fellows that I ever knew, little Peter, at six years of age, was the quaintest and funniest.

Now, as this, like all the rest of my stories, is a "*real true*" story, I dare say you would like to know who Peter was, and where he lived—and, as I did not promise to keep it a secret, I will tell you. In the very first place, it will give you the most delightful feeling of interest in the world, and convince you that he was, or ought to have been, the happiest child possible, when you read that he lived on a beautiful island, very near New York, and in a beautiful place that was called "Clear Comfort."

You may be sure that "Clear Comfort" was not one of those grand, gloomy places, with forty cross old gardeners trotting about continually, and scratching at the walks with their rakes, and counting every flower in the beds, so that, if you happened to pick a lady's ear-drop, or a lady's slipper, or a white lily, or a red rose, as Peter often did, they would find it out immediately, and be ready to cut your head off. Not at all.

With occasional assistance for the rough work, Peter's *mother* was the gardener in this charming spot, and it really seemed as if the flowers loved her as much as she loved them, and grew up, under her beautiful hands and dainty care, in such profusion and splendor, as the cross old gardeners in the neighboring places would have given all their eyes and elbows to have beaten; but, unfortunately, they did not happen to have the winsome, coaxing ways, and sweet smile of Peter's mother; and I suppose the flowers knew it, and that was the reason why every thing in her garden was nine times handsomer than anywhere else.

The house Peter lived in was a long, low, one storied cottage, with dormer windows peeping up here and there, and every one of them in summer had an ornamental frame clinging around it, of scarlet-runners or some other beautiful vine. One night, one of Peter's sisters chanced to look through one of these windows as an artist was passing, and he declared that the maiden with her fair hair, and the blended roses of her cheek, in the frame of delicate leaves and flowers, so graceful and appropriate, were far more lovely and picturesque than any gold-bedecked portrait he had seen in the Academy of

Design.

All the rooms in this delightful cottage were exactly the right size, for you could have as many people in them at once as was just agreeable. Every room was filled with handsome, comfortable furniture, and the most beautiful things imaginable, besides; not such fine things as Mr. Marcotte, the French cabinet-maker, invents. Oh, no! they were far more wonderful and admirable; for there, in one corner, you would come upon a tiny bird's nest, the marvellous construction of which would fill you with admiration for the cunning little architect. Even Mr. Renwick, who built Grace Church and the Smithsonian Institute, could never make one like it if he tried all his life.

In another corner would be a few cotton bolls of sea-island cotton, the soft, snowy mass bursting from within, a perfect marvel to behold. Then Peter's father and sister would take long walks in the woods, and bring from thence great bunches of strange and splendid ferns, and wild flowers, growing unseen and unregarded, save by such refined and ardent admirers of Nature.

His elder sister sketched beautifully, and painted in water colors, and the walls were adorned with lovely little "bits" of landscape, so correctly drawn and softly tinted, that the eye delighted to rest upon them, and, altogether, "Clear Comfort" was just such a house as Washington Irving, N. P. Willis, Curtis, or any person of great taste and refinement would be enchanted to live in.

The waters of the Narrows streamed past the windows; opposite, were the lovely shores of Long Island, and beyond, the wide Atlantic Ocean. Every steamship and other vessel passed by so close, that if you waved your handkerchief, passengers were sure to return the politeness. Peter once waved a large cat at the Persia, as she went by in her stately grandeur, with flags flying in the sweet summer wind, and some one on board, seeing and enjoying the joke, held up a pig by the ears by way of return, and Peter ran into the house laughing, and declared to his sister that he heard it "creek," by which queer word, he meant "squeak."

One morning Peter jumped out of his little crib, which was close to his mother's bed, and felt in such excellent spirits, that he turned to his mother, and cried, "Do wake up, mamma! wake up, papa! it is so pleasant! I could jump out of the window with joy. I will, *too!*" and before his mother could spring from the bed to prevent him, Peter had scrambled out of the window, and was running along the eaves, his one little garment fluttering behind him in the soft summer breeze. He came presently to the window of his sister Minnie's room, and, as it was open, jumped in, and commenced dancing about and turning somersets in a perfect ecstasy of delight, exclaiming, "I am so happy! I am so happy! I don't know what to do! I wish I could sit up the whole time, and never go to bed any more, or have to spell long words, or learn that stupid multi-something-cation table; but just eat lumps of sugar, and play the whole time."

"Why, Peter!" said Minnie, who was now awake, and laughing at his comical antics, "I don't think it very likely you will ever die of learning. What are you going to do when you grow up, if you don't learn, while you are young, to read, write, and cipher?"

"Oh, there will always be plenty of people to read to me, just as there are now. I mean to hire two big girls to do nothing else but to read to me; when one is tired, the other shall begin. Just look at my little white mouse, Minnie: I dare say it is nothing but hard work, and that dreadful studying, that has turned his hair white! I mean to take care of my health, my dear," and the queer little fellow shook his head at her in a solemn fashion, looking at least fifty, and then scampered off to his mother's room to be dressed.

While the dressing was going on, Peter saw a spider, and exclaimed, "Only look, mamma! at that great daddy long-legs staring in at the window! I should think his legs were about two miles long. And, see! he has four tails sticking out behind!"

"Two inches would be nearer, Peter," answered his mother, "and his tails are all legs. I expect he is looking in to invite some poor little lady-fly into his parlor, and when he has her there, he will pounce upon his company and eat her up."

"The hateful thing!" exclaimed Peter; "I'll just tie a string to one of his legs, and throw him into the water. I've a first-rate string in my pocket. But here! what's the matter? what ails my pantaloons? where's my pockets?" he continued, looking down in dismay at the strange, baggy appearance of the garment.

The truth is, Peter's mother had been so busy looking at the spider, that she had put on and buttoned his pantaloons the wrong side before.

Peter went on saying, "Why, mother, what's a fellow to *do*? How am I to get my hands in my pockets?" He twisted his head over his shoulders till he made a terrible kink in his neck, and turned his arms nearly out of their sockets in his efforts to dive into his pockets; and there came over his childish face such a ridiculously solemn and tragical air, that his mother nearly died of laughter.

When she could speak she said, "You must excuse me, Peter, it was an accident. It is very fortunate your head don't come off. If I had buttoned *that* the wrong side before, you would have been worse off than a crab; they walk sideways, but you would have had to have walked backwards."

In a few moments the pantaloons were danced off, and put on again; this time "all right and tight," as Peter said. Then his mother washed his face and hands, till they perfectly shone, they were so bright and clean; and, at his earnest request, she brushed his hair very carefully, with a seam down behind, and a flourishing curl on top, "like the dandies."

And now the little boy's face assumed a serious, thoughtful expression, as, kneeling by the side of his good mamma, he repeated this little prayer:—

> "Ere from my room I wend my way,
> God grant me grace my prayers to say:
> O God! preserve my mother dear,
> In strength and health, for many a year;
> And O! preserve my father, too,
> And may I pay him reverence due;
> And may I my best thoughts employ,
> To be my parents' hope and joy:
> And O! preserve my sisters dear,
> From every hurtful influence here:
> And may we always love each other,
> Our sisters, father, and our mother;
> And still, O Lord, to me impart
> An innocent and grateful heart,
> That, after my last sleep, I may
> Awake to thy eternal day."[A]

> [A] S. T. Coleridge.

After saying this beautiful prayer he ran down stairs, and out into the sweet, fresh air, and had a glorious scamper, which gave him a famous appetite for his breakfast.

I am obliged to tell you that my little friend Peter was as full of mischief as an egg is full of meat, and he always went so seriously to work, with such a grave twinkle in his bright, blue eyes, that you could not help laughing if you were ever so angry.

One morning he was alone in the parlor, sitting in his little arm-chair; a pair of old spectacles, which he had picked up somewhere, perched on the end of his little nose, and one leg nursed up on the other, "just like grandpa," as he said. He was pretending to read the newspaper.

Presently he rose up, stretched his little legs, (and very fine legs they were,) the stockings upon which were tightly gartered above the knee, and pushing the spectacles up on the top of his forehead, as he had seen his grandfather do, he said to himself, "Dear me! very little news in the paper to-day! Only the quarantine burned down. I wish *I* had been there! What fun! to run all round with my little pail full of water, and help to put it out! I wish they would set something else on fire in the day time, and give a *man* a chance to see it! I wonder what I shall do next?" and Peter approached the window and looked out.

It was a still, lovely day; the sun sailed slowly up in the heavens, and the blue and rippling waters caught his richest beams. Numerous crafts crept lazily along, their snowy sails looking, in the distance, like the listless wings of great white birds resting upon the waves. Upon the pillars of the piazza the vines hung in rich festoons, and the naked arms of one great tree near by (which, from some cause, was dead) were perfectly covered with a prodigal and splendid flowering vine, presenting a strange but graceful and beautiful appearance, a monument to the exquisite and subtle taste which had spared it for this purpose.

Peter, young as he was, felt the witching influence of this lovely scene. He watched, with intense interest, a flock of birds high up in the heavens, wheeling swiftly round, and darting here and there, happy, joyous and free; and then he turned to look at a little singing bird of his sister's, imprisoned in a cage, hanging in the window.

"Well," said Peter, "it is a real shame to lock up this little bird, when its father and mother, uncles and aunts, godfathers and godmothers, and ever so many cousins, are running about in the sky, doing exactly as they please— that's a fact! I'll just let him out," and he opened the door of the cage.

In an instant the little bird flew out, darted through the window, and was lost in the distance. When he had watched until it had disappeared, Peter looked at the cage, and his face grew blank. All at once he began to think it barely possible that his sister would not be quite as delighted at the loss of her bird as he had at first fancied. To be sure this was a free country, but with certain reservations. He began to feel queer and frightened. "Goody! what shall I do?" he said to himself, burying his hands in his pockets, and standing in a contemplative attitude, with his chubby little legs very wide apart, the spectacles still on the top of his head, "Goody! Minnie will want to cut off all my fingers and toes for opening the door, I am sure she will! Oh! I know; I'll just go and catch a chicken, and put it in the cage; it will be all the same as the bird."

So the little scamp rushed into the kitchen for a handful of corn, and as the chickens were very tame, and clustered around him the moment he called them, he had no difficulty in capturing a small, white hen. Laden with his prize, Peter went, with a hop, skip and jump, back to the parlor, and by main force pushed and jammed the poor thing through the door of the cage, and shut it, and then sat down, his face excessively red, and breathing so hard you would have thought it was a porpoise come out of the water to make a call upon the family.

The chicken, meanwhile, was lifting up first one leg and then the other, in her very close quarters, with an expression of perfect astonishment and disgust—occasionally giving vent to her displeasure by a dismal "squawk," very unlike the sweet tones of a singing bird.

Peter thought the new bird might, perhaps, be hungry, and was scolding him about it; so he went again into the kitchen, and walked off with nearly a whole loaf of bread, which he crumbled in a great heap in a corner of the cage. The chicken only kicked it out in all directions over the carpet, and made a worse noise than ever, which plainly said, "I want to get out! I want to get out!"

Poor Peter felt that he was in a terrible scrape when he heard this abominable noise. I wish you could have seen his face when his sister Minnie came into the parlor, a few moments after, to practise her music. It was just the color of a stick of sealing wax or a fireman's shirt, and he looked frightened out of his five senses, and the whole of his wits.

At first she did not notice that any thing was amiss, as the piano was at the other end of the room, and she commenced playing a beautiful overture, when, suddenly, a loud, angry "cluck! cluck!" caused her to jump up, with a little scream.

Looking round at the cage, she exclaimed in great astonishment, "Why, what on earth! what is it? Has the bird got the dropsy and swelled out in that dreadful manner? Impossible! Goodness!" she exclaimed again, as the chicken gave vent to another cry, "It is not the bird at all!—it is a chicken. But how did it come there? Why, Peter! what a red face! Do you know, Peter? Answer me, this moment!"

And now poor little Peter fairly gave way. His lips, which had been trembling all the time she was speaking, were drawn down at the corners, nearly under his chin, as he sobbed out, "Why, Minnie, I thought the bird wanted to run up into the sky, where all the other birds were, so I just opened the door. I thought he would not go more than fifty miles, you know, and then come back you know! I am so sorry, Minnie, it is forty million pities if he *don't* come back. I put the chicken in the cage on purpose to please you; but she can't sing any thing but that old 'cluck, cluck!' and she kicked all the bread in my face, and I can't bear her. Oh, dear! oh, dear me!"

For her life Minnie could not help laughing, and, besides, she could not help admiring the brave manner (if he *did* cry about) with which her little brother told the truth. Peter was the baby of the family, an only son, and a great pet; but if he *was* dreadfully mischievous he never did a mean thing, *and never told a lie*! Think of *that*, boys and girls, and take example by the little fellow.

Minnie, when she saw how distressed he really was, generously forgave him, and bade good-by to her bird, though not without some tears, for she loved the little creature dearly; and to comfort Peter took him in her lap, and told him an entertaining story.

One day, his mother said, "I am going to New York for a few days; what shall I bring you, my darling, when I return?"

"Oh, mother! a penknife and a pair of skates for next winter, and a penknife! and a basketfull of lemons, to make lemonade! and—and—if you please, a penknife; do, please, mamma!"

His mother laughed at the great desire for a penknife, without which, all boys feel, I believe, that they are very much abused, and deprived of their peculiar right.

"I will remember all your wishes, my dear boy," she said, "particularly the penknife."

"Well, mamma, for fear you might forget, I will write you a letter, and papa shall take it to-morrow."

So that very afternoon, Peter took a large sheet of paper out of his mother's writing-desk, and, pressing his sister Alice into his service, dictated the following epistle:

"My Dear Darling Mamma,—I am very sorry you have gone away! very sorry, indeed; so I am, certainly. I have just bumped my head, and it hurts very much—not so very much, though—hardly any. I wish you were here, and, besides, I want to see you very much indeed. I want you to buy me a penknife. We have very pleasant weather here, and I hope you have pleasant weather in New York; I really *do* hope so, that's a fact, certainly. I 'spect you will buy me a penknife and a pair of skates.

"I wish I could come to see you; but, unluckily, I am too little, and, besides, I have no money, only but one penny; of course that would not do, as I have not enough money to go to and fro—of course not—I have only one penny.

"Have you money enough to buy my penknife? I have been a pretty good boy, except sometimes, when I was cross—sometimes, last night, when I wanted two pieces of cake; but I don't mean to be cross again, not that I know of—may be. I hope you will bring my penknife. I think that is long enough—of course it is. Good-by, my dear mamma. I hope you will come back soon, and bring my penknife the same day. Bring it in your pocket, shut up, with a paper round it, and tied, and I am your affectionate son,

"PETER."

"Shall I write a postscript?" said Alice.

"What's a postscript?" said Peter, with his head on one side.

"It is some thing very particular indeed, which ladies always put in after the letter is finished."

"Oh, yes!" cried Peter, "I'm the boy for a postscript—certainly, of course!"

"Well," said Alice, holding her pen over the paper.

"Well," repeated Peter, "Postscript, put *that*! Got that down?"

"Yes, all written beautifully!" answered Alice.

"Dear mamma, please *pertikerlary* to bring me a penknife and—" oh, Alice, "a pair of skates and a penknife!" and then the wonderful letter was finished and sent the next morning; and let me tell you, Peter's mother laughed over and enjoyed this letter more than she would have done the finest complimentary epistle from the President of the United States.

You may be sure that Peter got the penknife and his skates, too. With the first, like boys in general, he cut himself about once a day; but he did not care a button for that, but just had his finger tied up by one of his kind sisters, and marched off, without even making a wry face, with his precious knife in his pocket. The skates came, too; but, as there had been no ice as yet, Peter had only tried them on dry ground, which Alice told him was far the best and safest style of skating, and repeated, for his edification, Mother Goose's solemn poem of—

> "Three children sliding on the ice—
> All, on a summer's day—
> The ice was thin; they all fell in;
> The rest, they ran away.
> Now, had these children been at home,
> Or sliding on dry ground,
> Ten thousand pounds to one penny
> They had not all been drowned."

All of which was heathen Greek to Peter, or, as he called it, "Stuff!"

One day, soon after her return, Peter's mother took him with her to visit an excellent lady of her acquaintance, who lived near by. They found her sitting in the parlor, with her eldest son and daughter, looking over a new and beautiful book, called Melodies for Childhood. Soon after they were seated the lady said, "Something very amusing happened up-stairs just now. I have a friend here spending the day, who brought her little baby of four months with her. My little girl is just the same age. Of course my friend's baby must have her nap, and I gave her my little one's cradle to sleep in. But my baby was so very much put out at this that she could not sleep at all; and little Harry, who, as you know, is not quite three years old, was so grieved at what he supposed was the wickedness of the other baby, in taking away his sister's property, that he marched up to the cradle—his little breast heaving, his eyes flashing, and his hand raised, while, with high, indignant voice, he asked, *Mamma, sall I* SAPP *her?*" and I had to run to save the little innocent from the impending blow."

Peter listened to all this with very large eyes and all the ears he had, which were only two, and quite small; and when Harry came into the room, a moment after, he rushed up to him, in a prodigious hurry, and cried, "Harry, did you slap her? I would! Let's both go up-stairs and do it now. Give it to her like sixty, for sleeping in your sister's bed!" This proposal so delighted Harry that, in turning round suddenly to go out, he fell over a chair and bumped his nose. Fortunately, this accident kept both the children in the room, and the slapping of the baby had to be postponed.

In the winter time, on the island, the ladies hold sewing meetings, and sew for the poor; and many a warm garment and nice hood is made, and given away to those who otherwise would suffer from the bitter cold.

The pleasantest of these meetings, every one said, was at "Clear Comfort." They, all seemed to feel and acknowledge the sweet spell of the place; and then, Minnie made such wonderful cakes, and the hot biscuit were so light and feathery, that it certainly was the very clearest comfort and enjoyment to eat them, and an inducement to sew ever so much faster afterwards.

It was at one of these delightful meetings that I first met Peter, sitting in front of the splendid wood fire in his own little arm-chair, with his kitten in his lap and a demure twinkle in his blue eye, but not in the least abashed at being the only gentleman in the party.

It was perfectly surprising how many kisses were bestowed upon Peter, and how like a matter of course he took them, and how like a real little gentleman he answered all the questions the ladies asked him; which so delighted a very short, brown lady that she wanted to give him a houseful of books and toys; but, not being quite able to afford that, she sent him on last Christmas eve some stories she had written many years before, accompanied by this string of rhymes, each verse of which must be read in *one* breath; and, as taking long breaths is beneficial to the lungs, I may as well say that this is about all the merit they have. Here it is. Peter calls it his "Pottery" letter:—

I.

My dear little Pēt-
Er, so very neat,
With such tiny feet
As can't well be beat;
And dressed up so sweet
That it's quite a treat
To walk up the street,
And take a cool seat

Away from the heat,
On purpose to meet
And kindly to greet
(Almost wishing to eat)
This dear little Pete,
Who lives in the mansion
Called "Comfort Complete."

II.

And now only look!
I send you this book
By Dinah, the cook,
Who is black as a rook;
And she's *undertook*,
By hook or by crook,
Or by crook or by hook,
To take you this book;
And she shall be *shook*
If she says she's *mistook*,
And to the wrong Peter
Has given this book.

III.

I do not affect
To be quite correct,
But I've *tried* to collect
These stories direct;
Which you may reject,
If the least disrespect,
Or the smallest neglect,
Or word incorrect
On the subjects elect
You can ever detect.
And please recollect,
That you may suspect
That I wish to protect,
And keep quite select,
My stories for children
I love and respect.

IV.

Then, what will you do?

Why, you'll tie up one shoe;
Then another—that's two
You'd begun to undo;
For all the world knew
You were sleepy "a few."
And looking askew
At the cat, who said "Mew!"
Meaning "Good-night," to you.
You'll wake up anew,
And say, "Mamma, who
Sent this book on view?
Have you the least clue?
I'm afraid she's a shrew,
As the color is blue.
The stories are true,
I supposes; don't you?"

V.

Then she'll say, "My dear,
'Tis Aunt Fanny, I hear.
She's nothing to scare,
For she's little and spare:
She's not very fair,
And as high as a chair."
Then you'll put on an air—
For in this affair
You have a great share—
And say, "I don't care
If she's *not* very fair,
And so little and spare,
Or as cross as a bear:
I protest and declare
I like her, now—there!"

VI.

And now, Peter, attend!
To me your ear lend.
Your little head bend,
My dear little friend!
And never pretend
You don't comprehend;
But just condescend,

For a very good end,
That face to unbend,
Those fingers extend;
And, smiling, commend
And, frowning, defend
This book that I send.
Say, "Sir, your opinion
You're asked to suspend."

VII.

Then I'll say, "Where'er
You go, and, whene'er
At 'Clear Comfort,' whate'er
You do, and howe'er,
The writer will ne'er
From her inmost heart tear
Little Peter; but wear
A sweet souvenir there
Of her little friend dear,
Which no one shall share
As long as she's here."

This "Pottery" pleased Peter very much, and he kept his sisters busy reading the stories in the little book to him.

As Peter is only six years old at present, I cannot possibly tell you the whole of his history; but I will keep my eye upon him all this coming year, and next Christmas, if you like, I will make another story about his funny doings and sayings; or, if you prefer, you can make his acquaintance, personally, in that charming place called *Clear Comfort*.

THE STORY TOLD TO WILLIE.

"Oh, dear mamma!" said Willie, one pleasant summer's afternoon, "do, please, tell me a story—ah, d-o!" and the little fellow put up his rosy mouth and kissed his mother; well knowing that she could not resist his entreaty, backed by so sweet a bribe. What mother can?

"Oh, you little rogue!" answered his mother, returning the caress, "I have told you every story I can recollect, at least twenty times each. Why not run out in the garden with your nice new ball, lying there on the floor, and see how high you can throw it up in the air? You must take more exercise in the open air, my dear little Willie. Let us make a bargain. If you will play half an hour, and come in with a pair of rosy cheeks, I will try to have a story ready for you—a *new* story."

"Shake a Paw on it."

"Oh, delightful!" cried Willie, and—accustomed to give his mother *instant* obedience—he caught up his ball and ran off, to obey her, with a sweet, pleasant expression in his face.

Dear little children, it makes such a wonderful difference how you obey your parents. If a boy is requested by his mother to leave his play and go upon an errand for her, and he goes slowly, making dreadful faces, and muttering to himself, "Dear me, why couldn't she send some one else; I *hate* to go!" do you think he gives his mother as much pleasure as when he says, "Yes, mamma, of course I will!" and runs off to do her bidding with two pleasant dimples in his cheeks? Which is the best way? I think Willie knew. Do you?

Willie was an only child. He had large blue eyes, fair curling hair, and dimpled cheeks; but I am sorry to say his cheeks were pale, for his constitution was very delicate, and, though a frolicksome little fellow, he very soon tired of play, and his greatest pleasure was to sit by his mother and listen to some interesting story.

Solomon has written in the Good Book that "even a child is known by his doings, whether his work be pure, and whether it be right." Children should never forget this. Willie tried to remember it; for he was so obedient, so thoughtful, and so loving, that I am sure, if he is permitted to live, he will grow up a good man.

While Willie was playing, his kind mother, true to her promise, went into the next room, where was a large book-case, to try and find some story that would interest and amuse her little son. Presently she opened a book, in which she chanced upon a story which she thought she could so simplify to his childish understanding as to interest him exceedingly. At this moment, Willie came bounding in—a delicate bloom on his cheeks, and his blue eyes sparkling.

"Well, dear mamma," he cried eagerly, and catching his breath, "I have played ball till my breath is as short as my nose. Is that enough?"

"Quite enough," said his mother, laughing. "Come and sit down, and in a few minutes, I hope, your breath will grow as long as your arm. I think I have a very nice story for you. It is about a fox and some other animals. It was written by a great author. As it is written, it will be almost *too old* for a little fellow like you, but I will make it younger if I can."

"Oh, that will be excellent!" said Willie, sitting down by his mother and rubbing his hands in a great state of delight. "A fox—only think! Will he talk? I hope he will; and I hope there will be giants and fairies, and—and very good children, and very bad boys, and—oh, every thing!"

His mother laughed again, and said, "There are only animals in this story, but it is very long."

"That's perfect," cried Willie, "I could listen to stories all day and all night; I hope this will last twice as long as possible—I mean," continued he, as his mother laughed at "possible," "very long, indeed, you know."

And now he settled himself on his little bench by the side of his mother, and, folding his hands, fixed his blue eyes upon her face as she began:

THE WOOING OF MASTER FOX.

"Once upon a time two very respectable cats, of very old family, had an only daughter, so amiable and beautiful that she was quite the belle of the place."

"How 'belle?'" said Willie.

"Why, she was the best and most beautiful young lady, and received all the presents and attentions."

"Oh, yes!" said Willie.

"Her skin was of the most delicate tortoiseshell; her paws were smoother than velvet; and her fine, white whiskers were twelve inches long, at the least; and then, above all, her eyes, instead of being green, were a lovely hazel, and so gentle that it was quite astonishing in a cat.

"When she was about two years and a half old she was left an orphan— poor thing! with a large fortune. Of course, she had a great many lovers who wanted to marry her; but, without troubling you with all the rest, I will come at once to the two rivals—the dog and the fox.

"Now Beppo, the dog, was a handsome, honest, straightforward, affectionate fellow; and he knew it, for he said:

"'I don't wonder at my cousin's refusing Bruin the bear, and Gauntgrim the wolf. To be sure, they give themselves great airs, and call themselves "*noble*;" but what then?—Bruin is always in the sulks, and Gauntgrim always in a passion. A cat, of any sense, would lead a miserable life with them. As for me, I am very good-tempered—when I am not put out; and I have no fault, that I know of, except that of being angry, and growling when I am disturbed at my meals. I am young and very good-looking, fond of play and amusement; and, altogether, as amiable a husband as a cat could find in a summer's day. If she marries me, well and good; if not, I hope I shan't be so much in love as to forget that there are other cats in the world.'

"So saying, Beppo threw his tail over his back, and set off to see the cat, as gay as a lark in the spring.

"But the fox had heard him talking to himself—for a fox is always meanly peeping about, into holes and corners, and listening where he has no business —and he burst out a-laughing as soon as Beppo was out of sight.

"'Ho—ho, my fine fellow!' said he, 'not quite so fast, if you please; you've got the fox for a rival, let me tell you.'

"Now, the fox is a beast that can never do any thing without a mean trick; and the cunning fellow was determined to put Beppo's nose out of joint by arriving at the cat's house first. But this was no easy matter; for though Reynard—"

"Reynard?" said Willie.

"That was the fox's name. Reynard could run faster than Beppo for a little way, but he was no match for him in a long journey. 'However,' said Reynard to himself, 'those good-natured creatures are never very wise; I think I know how to fix him.' With that the fox trotted off, by a short cut in the woods, and, getting before the dog, laid himself down by a hole in the earth, and began to make such a dismal howling that you could have heard him a mile off.

"My poor little sister has fallen into this hole, and I can't get her out."

"Beppo, on hearing this dismal noise, was terribly frightened. 'See now,' said he, 'if the poor fox has not got himself into some scrape. Those cunning creatures are always in mischief; I'm thankful it never comes into my head to be cunning,' and the good-natured fellow ran off as fast as he could, to see what was the matter with the fox.

"'Oh dear! Oh murder!' cried Reynard, 'what shall I do, what shall I do? my poor little sister has gotten into this hole, and I can't get her out; she'll certainly be smothered,' and he burst out a howling again, more piteously than before.

"'But, my dear Reynard,' said Beppo, 'why don't you go in after your sister?'

"'Ah! oh! you may well ask that,' said the fox; 'but in trying to get in, don't you perceive that I have sprained my back, and can't stir? O dear me! what shall I do if my poor little sister gets smothered?'

"'Pray don't vex yourself,' answered Beppo, 'I'll get her out in an instant;' and with that he forced himself, with great difficulty, into the hole.

"No sooner did the fox see that poor Beppo was fairly in, than he rolled a great stone to the mouth of the hole, and fitted it so tight that Beppo, not being able to turn round and scratch against it with his fore paws, was made a close prisoner, poor fellow.

"'Ha, ha,' cried the wicked fox, laughing, outside; 'amuse yourself with my poor little sister, while I go and call you all sorts of bad names, to your cousin the cat.'

"Of course you know that the poor little sister was not in the hole; it was a mean falsehood of Reynard's, and the bad fellow trotted off, never troubling his head what became of the poor dog.

"When he arrived near the cat's house, he thought he would first pay a visit to a friend of his, an old magpie, that lived in a tree, and knew every thing about every body. 'For,' thought Reynard, 'I may as well know the weak side of Mrs. Fox that is to be, before we are married.'

"'Why, how do you do?' said the magpie, 'what brought you so far from home?'

"'Upon my word,' said the fox, laying his paw on his heart, 'nothing so much as the pleasure of seeing your ladyship, and hearing those agreeable stories which your ladyship tells so delightfully; but, to tell you a great secret —be sure it don't go further.'

"'Oh, certainly not! on the word of a magpie.'

"'Ah! of course, I should have recollected that a magpie never tells secrets,' said the fox, ironically, 'but, as I was saying, you know her majesty the lioness.'

"'Certainly,' said the magpie, with an air of great importance.

"'Well, she was pleased to fall in—that is to say, to—to—take a fancy to your humble servant, and the lion grew so jealous that I had to run like a lamplighter to save my life. A jealous lion is no joke, let me assure your ladyship. But mum's the word.'

"Such a fine piece of news delighted the magpie, who was the greatest tell-tale in the world, so in return she told Reynard all about Bruin and Gauntgrim, and then she began to say all manner of unkind and ill-natured things about the poor young cat. She did not spare a single fault, you may be sure. The fox listened with all the ears he had, and he learned enough to convince him that the cat was rather vain and very fond of flattery.

"When the magpie had finished her ugly speech she said: 'But, my dear Mr. Reynard, you are very unfortunate to be banished from so splendid a court as that of the lion.'

"'Oh! as to that,' answered the fox, 'I feel some consolation, for his majesty made me a handsome present at parting; namely, three hairs from the inside of the ninth leg of the amoronthologosphorus. Only think of that, ma'am.'

Willie laughed at this long word.

"'The *what*?' cried the magpie, cocking down her left ear.

"'The amoronthologosphorus.'

"'La!' said the magpie, 'and what is that tremendous long word, my dear Mr. Reynard?'

"'The amoronthologosphorus is a beast that lives on the top of the North Pole, fifteen miles from any water, and the same distance from any land; it has nine legs, and on the ninth leg are three hairs, and whoever has those three hairs can be young and beautiful for ever.'"

"Dear me," said Willie, "I wish I could get those three hairs for my dear grandma."

"So do I," answered his mother, "and the magpie wanted them, too, for she exclaimed: 'Bless me, I wish you would let me see them,' and she poked out her claw for the three hairs.

"'Really, ma'am, I would oblige you with pleasure,' said the wicked fellow, who had no hairs, and never heard of the animal with the long name, 'but it is as much as my life is worth to show them to any but the lady I marry. But you'll be sure not to mention it.'

"'A magpie gossip, indeed!' cried the old tell-tale.

"The fox then wished the magpie good-night, and retired to a hole to sleep off the fatigues of the day, as he meant to present himself to the beautiful cat as fine as a Broadway dandy.

"The very next morning (nobody knew how) it was all over the place that Reynard had been banished from the lion's court, who, to console him, had made him a present of three hairs, that would magically convert the one that he married, even if she was a perfect scarecrow, into a young and beautiful lady for ever."

"It was the magpie that told, wasn't it?" asked Willie.

"I suspect it was," answered his mother, "and the cat was the very first to learn the news, and she was perfectly crazy to see so interesting a stranger, with three such wonderful hairs. 'I tell you what!' she said to her maid, 'I'll have those three hairs before I am three days older.'

"Then the cat put on a white satin bonnet with ten ostrich feathers fastened all over it, and a thread-lace veil, her pink satin shoes, and a green parasol, and set out for a walk. Of course, she met the fox the very first thing; and he made her such a low bow that he very nearly cracked his spine. She blushed, and simpered, and thought the fox was the very pink of politeness; and he flattered her until she was quite ready to believe he was, also, the pink of perfection.

"Meanwhile, let us see what became of his rival, poor Beppo."

"Ah, the poor fellow!" cried Willie, "no chance for him—buried alive! just think."

"Wait till the end. When Beppo found that he was in this dismal trap, he gave himself up for lost. In vain he kicked, and scratched, and banged his hind legs against the heavy stone, he only succeeded in bruising his paws; and, at length, he was forced to lie down, so exhausted that his tongue hung a quarter of a yard out of his mouth, and he breathed like a locomotive. 'Dear me!' he said, 'it won't do to be starved here, without trying my best to escape;' and he repeated to himself this fine piece of poetry, the comfort and truth of which he had often, proved:—

> "'If you find your task is hard,
>   Try—try again;
> Time will bring you your reward;
>   Try—try again.
> All that other dogs can do,
> Why, with patience, should not you?
>   Only keep this rule in view— TRY—
>   TRY AGAIN.'

"'Now, let me see—if I can't get out one way, I will try if there is not a hole at the other end.' Thus saying, his courage returned, and he began to push on in the same straightforward way in which he had always conducted himself. At first the path was exceedingly narrow, and he was squeezed almost as flat as a pancake, besides being in mortal fear that his ribs would be broken in pieces like a crockery tea-pot, the stones that projected on either side were so sharp and rough. If he had been a cat, it would not have made so much difference, as they are said to have nine lives. But Beppo persevered, and, at last, was rewarded; for, by degrees, the way became broader, and he went on with great ease and comfort till he arrived at a large cavern, and beheld an immense griffin sitting on his tail and smoking a huge pipe.

"What a fright poor Beppo was in! for the monster had only to open his mouth, to swallow him up, without pepper or salt, as easily as you would an oyster. However, he put a bold face upon the danger, and walking respectfully up to the griffin, he made a very low bow, and said, 'Sir, I should be very much obliged to you, if you would inform me how to find the way out of these holes into the world again?'

"The griffin took the pipe out of his mouth, and looked at Beppo as sharp as a carving-knife.

"'Ho, wretch!' said he, 'how did you come here? I suppose you want to steal my treasure; but I know how to treat such vagabonds as you, and I shall certainly eat you up.'

"'You can do that if you choose,' said Beppo, 'but it would be very unhandsome conduct in an animal forty times bigger than myself. For my own part, I never attack a dog that is not of my own size: I should be very much ashamed of myself if I did. And as to your treasure, I am an *honest* dog, sir, as is very well known, and would not touch it if it was all composed of marrow-bones.'

"'Upon my word,' said the griffin, who could not help smiling, for the life of him, 'you are very free, and rather saucy; but, I say, how did you come here?'

"Then the good fellow, who did not know what a lie was, (I hope all the boys and girls reading this can say the same,) told the griffin his whole history —how he had set off to see his cousin the cat, and how that scamp of a Reynard had entrapped him into the hole.

"When he had finished, the griffin said to him, 'My friend, I see that you know how to speak the truth. I am very much in want of just such a servant as you will make me; therefore, stay with me, Beppo, and keep watch over my treasure when I sleep.'

"'Hum! two words to that,' said the dog. 'You have hurt my feelings very much by calling me a thief; and, besides, I am perfectly wild with impatience to go back to the wood to thrash that scoundrel the fox. I do not wish to serve you, even if you *gave* me all your treasures; so I beg you to let me go, and to show me the way to my cousin the cat.'

"'Look here, old fellow,' answered the griffin, 'I am not very fond of making speeches a mile long, and I give you your choice—be my servant, or (in a terrible voice) BE MY BREAKFAST; it is just the same to me. I give you time

55

to decide till I have smoked out my pipe, and that's the short and the long of it.'"

"What a cruel old griffin!" exclaimed Willie; "why didn't he catch an elephant, and eat him instead of the dog? Suppose it had been me, mamma, what would I have done?"

"Just what Beppo did, my dear, for the weak must yield to the strong, in a case where life can be saved without sin. So the dog said to himself, 'Of course, it is a dreadful misfortune to live in a cave with this abominable old griffin; but, perhaps, if I do my duty and serve him faithfully, he will take pity on me, some day, and let me go back to the world and tell my cousin what a good-for-nothing rogue the fox is; and, besides, though I would fight like forty Indians or General Jackson, it is impossible to conquer a griffin, with a mouth of so monstrous a size—it is twice the size of a barn-door.' In short, he decided to stay with the griffin.

"'Shake a paw on it,' said the grim old smoker, and the dog shook paws.

"'And now,' said the griffin, 'I will tell you what you are to do—look here;' and, moving his great fan-like tail, he showed the dog an enormous heap of gold and silver, in a hole in the ground, that he had covered with the folds of his tail; and, also, what the dog thought far more valuable, a great heap of bones, of very delicious smell and appearance.

"'Now, old fellow,' said the griffin, 'in the day-time I can take very good care of these myself; but, at night, I am so tired that I can't keep my eyes open, so when I sleep you must watch over them, as if you had fifty-nine eyes.'

"'Very well,' said the dog, 'I'm the boy for watching! and as to the gold and silver, they will be as safe as a bank; but I would rather you would lock up the bones, for they smell very nice, and, as I am often hungry of a night, I am afraid—'

"'Hold your tongue,' interrupted the griffin, looking as cross as two sticks, and in a voice like a cannon going off.

"'But, sir,' said the dog, after a short silence, 'I am sure nobody ever comes here: who are the thieves, if I may be so bold as to ask?'

"'Well, I will tell you,' answered the griffin. 'In this neighborhood there are a great many serpents, regular anacondas, and, though they haven't a leg to stand on, they are always rearing up, looking over their own shoulders, and trying to steal my treasure; and if they caught me napping, they would sting me to death before you count five; so I have to keep one eye open all night, and I am almost worn into holes.'

"'You don't say so,' said the dog; 'well, I don't envy you your treasure, sir.'

"When the night came, the griffin, who was a very cute fellow, and saw that the dog was so perfectly honest that he was to be entirely trusted, laid down to sleep, and was soon snoring like twenty fat aldermen rolled into one, and Beppo, shaking himself almost out of his skin, so as to be quite awake, took watch over the treasure. His mouth watered till it made quite a pond at his feet, at the delightful bones, and he could not help smelling at them now and then; but the honest fellow said to himself, 'A bargain's a bargain, and since I have promised to serve the griffin, and shaken paws on it, I must serve him as an honest dog ought to serve.'"

"What a good dog!" said Willie; "I like him."

"In the very middle of the night, a great snake came creeping in by the side of the cave, but the dog spied him, and set up such a barking that you would have thought a whole pack of the largest fire-crackers was going off all at once. The griffin woke up with a start, and the snake crept away with all his might and main. Then the griffin was very much pleased, and he gave the dog one of the delicious bones to eat; and every night the dog watched the treasure, and did it so well, that not a single snake would have dared to poke its nose (if it had one) into the cave, and the griffin grew so fat, with the excellent rest he enjoyed, that he could hardly see out of his eyes, and his three double chins shook like a bowl of jelly.

"When we try to do our duty faithfully we are more comfortable than we expect, even if the duty is disagreeable. It happened so with our friend Beppo. The griffin regularly gave him an elegant bone for supper, which did not need mustard to make it relishing, and pleased Beppo more than a houseful of sugar-candy; and, pleased with his honesty, made himself as agreeable as it was possible for a savage old griffin to do. Still the poor dog was very anxious to return to the world, for, having nothing to do all day but to doze on the ground, he dreamed all the time of his beautiful cousin the cat; and, in fancy, he gave the rascal Reynard as hearty a worrying as a fox ever had from a dog's paws. But, alas! when he awoke panting, it was nothing but a dream.

"One night, as he was watching as usual over the treasure, what was his surprise, to see a most beautiful little black and white dog enter the cave: it came fawning to our honest friend, wagging its tail with pleasure."

"'Ah! little one,' said Beppo, 'you had better make tracks out of this place, I can tell _you_. See—there is a great griffin asleep in that corner over yonder, and if he awakes he will eat you up in half a second, or make you his servant, as he has made me.'

"'I know all that very well, my dear friend,' said the little dog, 'and I have come down here on purpose to deliver you. The stone is taken away from the mouth of the cave, and you have nothing to do but to go back with me. Come, dear brother, come,' and the little dog put on an air of entreaty very hard to resist.

"Poor Beppo was in the greatest state of excitement at this speech, and the pleading look, but he said: 'Don't ask me, for goodness' sake, my dear little friend; I would give every thing I have, except the wag of my tail, to escape out of this dismal cave, and roll on the soft grass once more; but if I leave my master the griffin, those abominable scamps of serpents, who are always on the watch, will come in and wriggle off his treasure, and, besides, sting him to death. I cannot go. Oh dear! I cannot go! I must, and I *will* be faithful.'

"Then the little dog came up close to Beppo, and put his fore paws round his neck, and looked into his eyes with his large lustrous orbs, and licked his face (which is all the same with dogs as kissing); and then gently taking his ear in his mouth, endeavored to draw him away from the treasure; but honest Beppo would not stir a step, though his heart beat, and he longed to go."

"At length the little dog, finding it all in vain, said: 'Well, then, if I *must* leave, at least shake paws for good-bye; but let me tell you, I have become so hungry, in coming down all this way after you, and talking so much, that I do wish you would give me one of those bones: dear me! how good they smell; come, give me one—that's a good fellow; one will never be missed.'

"'Alas!' said the good Beppo, 'how unlucky I am to have eaten up the bone my master gave me! I would have given it to you, and have gone without with the greatest pleasure. But I cannot give you one of these; my master made me promise to watch over them all, and I have given him my paw on it: it would be stealing. Me steal? never! I am sure a little dog of your respectable appearance will say nothing more about it.'

"Then the little dog got into a pet and turned very red—only the hair prevented one's seeing it—and spoke loud, as people in pets do, and said: 'Pooh! pshaw! what stupid nonsense you talk! just as if a great griffin would miss a little bone; perfect stuff!' and, nestling his little black nose under Beppo, he tried to bring up one of the bones."

"What a look the good Beppo gave him! it ought to have almost cut him in two: *he* grew angry now, and seized the little dog by the nape of the neck, and threw him about ten feet off, though without hurting him. And now what do you think happened?"

"W-h-a-t," said Willie, snapping his eyes, and clapping his hands, for he was deeply interested. "W-h-a-t—did—happen?"

"Why suddenly, like a flash, the little dog changed into a monstrous serpent, bigger than the griffin—his skin was all the colors of the rainbow, and, as he stuck out his long forked tongue, he hissed like a whole army of geese. Beppo was desperately frightened, and, though his heart beat like the thumping of the waves on a shore, he barked with all his might—great deep-mouthed barks, which woke the griffin immediately. He rose up in a great hurry, and the serpent immediately reared his crest and sprang upon him like lightning. Oh! what a horrible battle began! how the griffin and the serpent coiled and twisted themselves into double bow-knots, and bit, and darted their fiery tongues at each other! All at once, the serpent got uppermost, and was about to plunge his sharp and poisoned fangs into that part of the griffin's body which is unprotected by scales, when Beppo rushed to him, and, seizing him by the tail, gave him such a tremendous bite, that he could not help turning round to kill his new assailant, and then the griffin, taking advantage of the opportunity, caught the serpent by the throat, with both claws, and fairly strangled him.

"As soon as he had recovered his breath and composure, he heaped all manner of caresses on Beppo for saving his life. Beppo told him the whole story, and the griffin then explained that the dead serpent was the king of all the serpents, and had the power to change himself into any shape he pleased. 'If he had tempted you,' said he, 'to leave the treasure for a single moment, or to have given him any part of it, even the little bone he begged for, he would have crushed you in an instant, and stung me to death while I slept; but I see, Beppo, none have power to hurt the *honest*.'

"'That has always been my belief,' answered Beppo. 'Honesty is the best policy, all the world over, and now, sir, you had better go to sleep again, and I will watch as before.'

"'Thank you, my good fellow,' said the griffin, 'I have no longer any need of a servant, for now that the king of the serpents is dead, the rest will never molest me. It was only by his orders, and to get at my treasure, that they dared to brave the den of a griffin.'

"Upon hearing this, the dog was in a perfect ecstasy of delight, and standing on his hind legs and clasping his fore paws together, he made a most eloquent speech, enough to bring real tears into the eyes of a crocodile, and entreated the griffin to let him return to the world, to visit his cousin the cat, and worry his rival the fox.

"'Well, I am not ungrateful,' answered the griffin, 'you shall return, and I will teach you all the cunning tricks of our race, which is much more cunning than the race of that numskull the fox, so that you will be able to cheat him to your heart's content.'

"'Ah! excuse me,' said Beppo, hastily, 'I am just as much obliged to you, but I fancy honesty is a match for cunning any day; I would rather be a *dog of honor*, than to know and practise all the tricks in the world.'

"'Well,' said the griffin, making a wry face—for he was put out at Beppo's bluntness—'well, do as you please; it is all the same to me. Good-bye. Shake a paw. I wish you all possible success.'

"The griffin now opened a secret door in the side of the cavern, and the dog saw a broad path, that led at once into the woods. Before he went, he thanked the griffin with his paw on his heart, and wished him a long life and a merry one, and then ran off wagging his tail. It was a beautiful moonlight evening; and the sweet breath of the wild flowers, as the gentle wind went floating by, filled the dog's senses with delight; he was happy, because he was honest, and he said to himself as he trotted along, 'Ah! Mr. Fox, there's no trap for an honest dog, that has not two doors to it, smart as you think yourself.'"

"Oh! I am so glad he is out," cried Willie, clapping his hands; "go on, mamma, please."

"Why, my dear little boy," answered his mother, "do you know what time it is? the sun is setting," and she took out her watch. "Why, only see! after 7 o'clock! we must stop now. I had no idea we had been reading some and making up some of this story so long; come, little boy, time for your bread and milk; as the good dog is safe, we will bid him good-bye to-night, and I will read you the rest to-morrow."

"Dear Beppo, I love him," said Willie, skipping about the room; "I hope I shall always be an honest dog—an honest boy I mean," he continued, laughing. "How splendid to have every body trust you, and leave all kinds of treasure for you to take care of! Mamma, would you like me to take care of grandma's portrait? I know that is a great treasure: I would put it under my bed and stare at it all day."

"But what would you do at night?" said his mother, laughing.

"Oh!" said Willie, "to be sure! why, we must have a dog like Beppo, you know. I am the griffin, see how fierce I look!" and Willie looked so fierce, that his mother pretended to be terribly frightened, and ran away, Willie tearing after her, his blue eyes dancing with fun, and they were both having a fine scamper, when Willie's father stood laughing at the door.

And now tea was ready; Willie's tea was bread and milk. He never had rich cake, or sweetmeats, or strong tea, or hot bread, which are all very fine while you are eating them, but which create quite a riot in the stomach of a delicate child, and often lay the foundation of life-long indigestion. He had a mother who was really kind, and did her utmost to save him from bodily pain, and took unwearied pains in storing his mind with noble thoughts, a love of truth, and a contempt for every thing mean. Her almost hourly prayer was, that her only son and child might grow up to be a Christian—"to love God with all his heart, and his neighbor as himself"—and, so far, the dear little fellow had richly rewarded her care.

The next day Willie studied his lessons, and knew them perfectly, and played on the lawn before the house. Although more than once his eyes sparkled with impatience to hear the rest of the delightful story, he did not annoy his mother, as some children do, with such expressions as these: "Come, now—right away. I want to hear the rest of that story. Oh! dear me! how long you are! I—wish—you—would—COME." Oh, no; Willie knew that his dear mother had many things to do, and he did not say one word about Beppo till about the same time the next afternoon, as his mother took her seat by the large and pleasant window which looked out upon the lawn; then he went up to her, and put his arms round her neck, and kissed her as before, and said: "Mamma, Mr. Fowler, the Phrenologist, says you can tell all about a boy, by the bumps on his head. I think I must have a prodigious bump of liking to have stories read or told to me. I have thought all day about Beppo and the hateful old griffin; but I have not said any thing or teased you—have I, mamma? I have been as quiet as a drum with a hole in it—haven't I, mamma?"

"It hardly needs a tongue to understand you, my dear boy, your eyes talk so fast; and as to the bumps, there is one very large one of loving me, I am certain; for you are a good, thoughtful child, but rather a small one for wanting to scamper and frolic in the open air. Come, I will make the same bargain as yesterday; half an hour's exercise, and then the story."

"Certainly," said Willie, with a pleasant laugh; "if you asked me to stand on my head, I would do it, mamma—or try, any way. I wish your ladyship good afternoon for half an hour," and Willie put his feet together, turning out his toes, and made such a very low and polite bow to his mother, that he nearly tumbled on his nose, and then ran out on the lawn.

As his mother watched him, she smiled, and sighed, and said to herself, "If my little Willie were only stronger, every desire of my heart would be fulfilled;" and then she repeated to herself those pleasant words of Willis:—

"There's something in a noble boy—
　　A brave, free-hearted, careless one,
With his unchecked, unbidden joy—
　　His dread of books, and love of fun—
And in his clear and ready smile,
Unshaded by a thought of guile,
　　And unrepressed by sadness—
Which brings me to my childhood back,
As if I trod its very track,
　　And felt its very gladness."

When the half hour was over she called Willie, and he came bounding in—his cheeks flushed and his eyes sparkling; and it did not take long, let me tell you, to arrange his bench and sit close beside his mother, ready for the fine treat she had promised him.

"Where did I leave off, Willie?"

"Where the dog bade good-bye to the griffin, and came out in the moonlight," said Willie, whose memory was excellent.

"Yes. Well, Beppo now curled his tail, in the very last fashion, over his leg, and trotted off in fine style to the cat's house. When he was within sight of it, he stopped to take a drink and a bath in a pond near by; and who should be there, to be sure, but the old magpie!

"'And what do *you* want, friend?' said she, turning up her nose—for Beppo looked rather shabby after his confinement in the cave and his long journey.

"'I am going to see my cousin the cat,' answered he.

"'*Your* cousin—pretty well, indeed!' said the magpie; 'don't you know she is going to be married to Reynard the fox? This is not the time for her to receive the visits of a clumsy fellow like you.'

"These uncivil words put the dog in such a passion that he very nearly bit the magpie. Such bad news, too! It was too bad. But, keeping his temper—as dogs and every body else should always try to do—and *without answering* a word, he went, at once, to his cousin's residence.

"The cat had a beautiful house, full of comfortable arm-chairs, and sofas covered with pink satin. She kept a French cook, who prepared the most delicious dishes of mice and small birds, smoking hot, from morning till night; and you would think it rained cream, she had such a quantity always on hand. There was no water to be seen, for a cat hates water—though, strange to say, she is particularly fond of fish; and our cat would have had a broiled whale for breakfast, no doubt, if smaller fry were wanting—for she denied herself nothing.

"When Beppo arrived, the cat was sitting at the window trying to catch a fly. Her motions were so graceful, and she looked so beautiful, that Beppo lost his heart immediately. Never had he seen so charming a cat before. So he came up, wagging his tail at a great rate, and with his most amiable air; when the cat, getting up, shut the window in his face, and, lo! Reynard the fox appeared instead.

"'Come out here, you rascal!' growled Beppo, showing his teeth—'come out, I say, you mean fellow, and get what you richly deserve. I have not forgiven you your trick, and you see I am no longer shut up in a cave, or unable to punish your wickedness.'

"'Oh, go home, you silly fellow!' sneered the fox, 'you have no business here; and, as for fighting you—pshaw!' Then the fox left the window, and disappeared. But Beppo was dreadfully enraged, and began to kick and scratch at the door, and made such a racket that presently the cat herself came to the window.

"'How now?' she said, angrily, 'what do you mean by such rudeness? Who are you, and what do you want at my house?'

"'Oh, my dear cousin!' said Beppo, 'do not speak so severely; I have come here on purpose to pay you a visit, and to entreat you not to listen to that villain Reynard. You have no idea what a bad fellow he is.'

"'What!' said the cat, blushing, 'do you dare to abuse your betters in this fashion? I see very well you have a design on me. Go, this instant, or—'

"'Enough, madam!' said the dog, proudly,—for he was very much wounded—'you need not speak twice to me. I wish you good morning.'

"And he turned slowly away, and went under a tree, where he took up his lodgings for the night. But the very next morning there was a great excitement in the neighborhood. A stranger, of a very different style of travelling from that of the dog, had arrived in the middle of the night, and fixed his abode in a large cavern, hollowed out of a steep rock. The noise he made, in flying through the air, was so great that he had awakened every bird and beast in the parish; and such a twittering, and crowing, and barking, and mewing, and growling, and roaring were never heard in the night before, when honest folks are supposed to be sleeping. Reynard, whose bad conscience never let him sleep very soundly, put his head out of the window and perceived, to his great alarm, that the stranger was nothing less than a monstrous griffin.

"You must know that the griffins are the richest beasts in the whole world.

They perfectly roll in diamonds—not to speak of any quantity of marrow-bones; and that is the reason why, like misers, they keep so close at home. Whenever it does happen that they go to the expense of travelling, all the world is sure to know it, and talk about it.

"The old magpie was in the most delightful state of agitation. What could the griffin want? she would give her ears if any body could get at him to know, and, being determined to find out, she hopped up the rock, and pretended to be picking up sticks for her nest.

"Hollo! you are the very Lady I want to see."

"'Hollo, ma'am!' cried a very rough voice, and she saw the griffin putting his head out of the cavern. 'Hollo! you are the very lady I want to see; you know all the people about here, don't you?'

"'All the *best* company, your lordship, I certainly do,' answered the magpie, putting her head on one side, and dropping a very low courtesy.

"Then the griffin marched out, with great dignity, to smoke his pipe in the open air; and, blowing the smoke in the magpie's face, in order to set her quite at her ease, continued—

"'My dear madam, are there any respectable beasts of good family in this neighborhood?'

"'Oh dear! the most elegant society, I assure your lordship,' cried the magpie. 'I have lived here myself these ten years,' she continued, drawing up and trying to look twice her size, 'and the great heiress the cat yonder, attracts a vast number of strangers.'

"'Pooh! fiddlesticks!' said the griffin, 'much *you* know about heiresses; there is only one heiress in the whole world, and that is my daughter.'

"'Bless me! has your lordship a family? I beg you a thousand pardons, I thought you were a bachelor. I only saw your lordship's own carriage last night, and did not know you brought any one with you.'

"'My daughter went first, and was all settled before I arrived. She did not disturb you, I dare say, as I did, for she sails along like a swan; but I have the gout in my left claw, and am rather apoplectic, and that is the reason I puff and groan like an express engine, when I take a journey.'

"'Ah, indeed! quite sorry, I declare! Shall I drop in upon Miss Griffin, and see how she is after the fatigue of her journey?' said the magpie, walking up.

"'You are too kind, but I don't intend her to be seen while I stay here; she is such a wild young thing, I am afraid of the young beasts running away with her, if they once heard how very handsome she is; she is the very picture of me, but she is so terribly giddy! not that I should care, if she went off with a rich and fashionable young fellow, if I did not have to give her her fortune, which is enormous, and I don't like parting with money, ma'am, when I have once got it, that's a fact. Ha, ha! ho, ho!'

"'Dear me! you are too witty, my lord. But, if you refused your consent, what then?' said the curious magpie, who was crazy to know all about so grand a family.

"'Oh, I should have to pay it all the same, ma'am; it was left to her by her uncle, the dragon. But don't tell, I beg of you.'

"'Oh my! not for the world; your lordship may be quite easy. I wish your lordship a very good morning.'

"Away flew the magpie, and she did not stop till she got to the cat's house. The cat and the fox were at breakfast; they had cream, fricaseed chicken, stewed mice, fried oysters, boiled fish, roasted butterflies, baked grasshoppers, and frizzled frogs; a breakfast fit for a king. The fox was just making a tender speech, for he had his paw on his heart. 'Beautiful scene!' cried the magpie, which made the cat turn scarlet, and she invited the magpie to take a seat.

65

"Then off went the magpie's tongue, like a sewing machine, 'glib, glib, glib; chatter, chatter, chatter; clup, clup, clup; tick-a, tick-a, ticka.'"

This made Willie laugh. "What a tell-tale," he cried, rising up in his seat and bumping down again, two or three times.

"Yes, indeed," continued his mother, "for she did not stop till she had related the whole story of the griffin and his daughter, and ever so much besides, that the griffin had never told her.

"The cat listened with the greatest attention. Another young lady in the place, and richer than her—she felt a little jealous. 'But is Miss Griffin handsome?' said she, smoothing her beautiful long whiskers.

"'Handsome!' cried the magpie, 'O if you could only see the father! such a splendid mouth! a mile wide; such eyes! as yellow as an orange; and such a complexion! all manner of colors—and he declares she is the very image of him! But what do you say, Mr. Reynard? You, who have travelled so much, have, perhaps, seen the young lady.'

"'Why, I can't say I have,' answered the fox, who had been in a brown study; 'but she must be wonderfully rich! I dare say that jackanapes, the dog, will be making up to her.'

"'Ah! by the way, my dear,' said the magpie, 'what a fuss he made at your door yesterday; why would you not permit him to enter?'

"'Oh!' said the cat, looking very proper and demure, 'Mr. Reynard says he is a dog of very bad character—pretending to be good-natured, and then biting your nose off, if he can. Dear me! I hope he won't quarrel with you, dear Reynard.'

"'With me! O, the poor wretch, no! he might bluster a little; but he very well knows, that if I am once angry he is a goner—I should make mince meat of him; but I did not mean to boast of myself.'

"In the evening, Reynard would have given his ears to go to see the griffin, but what could he do? There was the dog, sitting under the opposite tree, watching for him, and Reynard had no wish to prove his boasted courage. But, as usual, he resolved on a trick to get rid of Beppo.

"A young buck of a rabbit, a sort of country beau, had called in upon his cousin the cat, to pay her his respects, and Reynard, taking him aside, said: 'Look here, my young friend, do you see that shabby-looking dog under the tree? Well, he has insulted the cat, your cousin, and you ought to punish him. In my situation, you know, I can do nothing; but if you do not notice it you will have that horrid old magpie calling you a coward.'

"The rabbit looked very foolish; he was a timid little fellow, and he did not want to fight; he told the fox he was no match for Beppo, and, although he was very fond of his cousin, he did not wish to interfere in her domestic affairs, and he tried every possible way to get out of the scrape; but the artful fox flattered him, and told him that Beppo was the biggest coward in the whole world, and would not fight, but would make him an humble apology, which would be a great feather in his (the rabbit's) cap, and at last the rabbit promised to go and ask the dog to fight.

"'Well,' said the fox, 'all right; go to the great field the other side of the woods, and I'll follow in half an hour; and, I say—hark! In case he does agree to fight, and you feel the least afraid, I'll be there and take it off your hands, with the greatest pleasure. Depend upon *me*, my dear sir.'

"Away went the rabbit. The dog was astonished at the great show of courage; but on hearing that the fox would be present, he consented in a moment to go. This did not gratify the rabbit very much; he went very slowly, and, seeing no fox there, his heart sank down to his paws; and while the dog had his nose to the ground to smell if the fox was coming, the rabbit took to his heels, slipped into a burrow, and left Beppo to walk back again.

"Meanwhile, the fox went softly to the rock; he looked about very carefully, for he had a notion that a griffin papa would not be very civil to foxes.

"There were two holes in the rock—one below, and one above; and while Reynard was peering about, he saw a great claw from the upper hole beckoning to him.

"'Ah! oh!' said the fox, 'that must be Miss Griffin;' so he approached, and a voice said: 'Charming Mr. Reynard, I am locked up in this dismal hole; do you not think you could contrive to deliver me?'

"'O goodness!' cried the fox, tenderly, 'what a beautiful voice, and ah! my poor heart, what a lovely claw! Is it possible that I hear the daughter of my lord, the griffin?'

"'Hush, flatterer! not so loud if you please. My father is taking a walk, and is very quick of hearing. He has tied me up by my poor wings in the corner, for he is terribly afraid of some one running away with me. You know, I have all my fortune settled on myself.'

"'Talk not of fortune,' cried the fox, 'but how can I deliver you? Shall I enter, and knaw the cord?'

"'Alas!' answered Miss Griffin, 'it is an immense chain I am bound with. However, you may come in and talk more at your ease.'

"The fox peeped all round, and seeing no sign of the griffin, he entered the lower cave, and stole up-stairs to the upper story; but, as he went on, he saw such immense piles of jewels and gold, and all sorts of treasure, that he did not wonder at the old griffin sneering at the cat's calling herself an heiress. He was so delighted with this wealth, that he entered the upper cave, resolved to consider Miss Griffin the most beautiful creature in the world.

"There was, unfortunately, a great chasm between the landing-place and the spot where the young lady was chained, and he found it impossible to pass. The cavern was very dark, but he saw enough of Miss Griffin's figure to perceive, in spite of her hooped petticoat, that she was the image of her father, and the most hideous scarecrow the earth ever saw.

"However, he concealed his disgust, and began to compliment her about her beauty, and did it so well, that she was, or pretended to be, enchanted with him. He implored her to run away with him the moment she was unchained.

"'That is impossible,' said she, 'you might as well ask me for a piece of my nose, for my father never unchains me except in his presence, and then I cannot stir out of his sight.'

"'The good-for-nothing wretch!' said Reynard; 'I wish the rocks would come down about his ears: what is to be done?'

"'Why, there is only one thing that I know of,' answered Miss Griffin, 'which is this: I always make his soup for him, and if I could mix something in it that would put him fast asleep, before he had time to chain me up again, I might slip softly down, and carry off all the treasure on my back.'

'Oh! delightful!' exclaimed Reynard, 'what invention! what wit! I will go and get some poppies, that will set him snoring directly.'

"'Alas!' sighed Miss Griffin, 'poppies have no effect upon griffins; the only thing that can ever put my father fast asleep, is a nice young cat boiled in his soup; it is perfectly astonishing what a charm it is. But where to get a cat? it must be a young lady cat, too!'

"Reynard was a little startled when he heard this; so very singular, that a boiled cat would put any one to sleep; but he thought that griffins were different from the rest of the world, and, of course, nothing was too hard to do to win such a rich heiress.

"'I know a cat, a maiden cat,' said he; 'but I feel rather unpleasant at the thought of having her boiled in the griffin's soup. Would not a dog do as well?'

"'Oh, you mean thing!' said Miss Griffin, pretending to weep, you love the cat; 'it's as plain to be seen as your ears; go and many her, and leave me here to die of grief!' and she began to cry and bo-hoo like ten hyenas.

"In vain the fox said that he did not care a straw for the cat; nothing now would satisfy her but a solemn promise that he would bring poor puss to the cave, to be boiled for the griffin's soup."

"Oh! what a bad, bad, wicked fox!" cried Willie; "if I knew how to fire a gun, I would shoot him—I would pull his tail off—I would give him soup made of stones and sticks—that I would!"

"Yes, he was a mean, wicked fellow," said his mother; "but wait till you hear the end." And now, Miss Griffin and he had a grand consultation, how they should entrap the poor cat, and Reynard said at last: 'The best way will be to put a basket out of the window, and draw it up by a cord; the moment it arrives at the window be sure to clap your claw on the cat, for she is terribly active.'

"'Fiddle!' answered Miss Griffin; 'I should think myself a goose, if I did not know how to catch a cat!'

"'It must be when your father is out,' said the fox.

"'Oh! certainly; he takes a walk, you know, every evening.'

"'Well, let it be to-morrow, then,' said Reynard, for he was impatient for the treasure.

"This being arranged, Reynard thought it time to make off; he stole down stairs and tried to steal some of the treasure by the way, but it was too heavy for him to carry, and he came to the conclusion, that to get the money he must take the lady, too.

"When he returned to the cat's house, and saw how plain every thing looked, after the jewels in the griffin's cave, he quite wondered how he had ever thought she was the least good-looking, but he concealed his wicked intention, and made himself particularly agreeable.

"'Only guess where I have been!' said he. 'To our new neighbor, the griffin —a most charming person. As for that silly magpie, she told a tremendous fib —for he has no daughter at all. He has heard of your beauty, my dear, and, on my telling him we were going to be married, he insisted upon giving a great ball and supper, in honor of the event, and I have accepted the invitation.'

"'Oh! dear! of course,' said the pretty creature, who felt highly delighted. 'I shall wear my white satin with the lace flounces, and, no doubt, he will ask me to be his partner, when we dance the Lancers.'

"'And only think! what a delicate attention,' said the fox. 'As all his treasure is on the ground floor, he gives the ball in the second story, so he will hang a basket out for the company, and draw them up with his own claw—how condescending!'

"The cat, who had never been much in society, was almost crazy with delight, at the prospect of going to such a grand party, and talked of nothing else. When the evening came, the fox, looking out of the window, saw his old friend Beppo, watching for him as usual. 'Ah! that torment! I had quite forgotten him; what is to be done now? If he once gets hold of me, I shall be a dead fox in five minutes after.'

"But, as usual, the fox thought of a cunning trick; he desired the cat to set out first, and to wait for him at the corner. 'You just leave the door open,' said he, 'and I will follow directly.'

"When the cat made her appearance, Beppo walked up to her very humbly, and begged her to allow him to say a few words to her; but Reynard had so poisoned her mind against him, that she made her back up into an arch, and I am sorry to say, with an action that looked very much like spitting, went past him without answering. Ah! how angry it made him with Reynard; but his rage was changed to joy, when he saw that the cat had left the door open. 'Now, wretch!' thought he, 'you cannot escape me.' So he walked in quickly, at the door; but what was his surprise, to see Reynard lying down, panting, as if his heart would break, and rolling his eyes, as if he was in the very worst kind of fit.

"'Oh! my friend,' he said, in a weak, trembling voice, 'I am dying; put your paw upon mine, and say you forgive me.'

"In spite of his anger, Beppo was so good and generous, that he could not bite a dying enemy.

"'You served me a very mean trick. You left me to starve in a hole, and you have made my cousin dislike me; I meant to punish you, but if you are really dying, that alters the affair.'

"'Oh! oh!' groaned the fox, 'I am past help; the cat has gone for doctor Ape, but he'll never come in time. What a thing it is to have a bad conscience on one's death-bed. But wait till the cat returns, I will do you justice with her, before I die.'

"The good-natured dog was very sorry to see his enemy in such a dismal state, and he did his best to console him.

"'Oh! oh!' said the fox, 'I am burning with fever,' and he hung his tongue out till you could nearly see the roots, and rolled his eyes, till they nearly came out of the top of his head.

"'Is there no water here?' said Beppo, looking round.

"'Alas, no!—yes, now I think of it, there is some in that hole in the wall; but it is so high I cannot climb in my weak state; and I dare not ask you, whom I have injured so much.'

"'Don't mention it,' said Beppo; 'but the hole's very small, I could not put my nose through it.'

"'I know that; but if you climb up on that stone, and thrust your paw into the hole, you can dip it into the water, and so cool my poor parched tongue. O! what a thing it is to have a bad conscience.'

"The good dog sprang upon the stone, and, getting on his hind legs, thrust his fore paw into the hole, when, suddenly, Reynard pulled a string that he had concealed under the straw, and Beppo's paw was fastened up tight, in a running noose.

"'You villain,' said he, turning round; but the fox leaped up gayly from the straw, and tying the string to a nail in the other end of the room, walked out, crying: 'Good-bye, my dear friend, I hope you'll enjoy yourself.' So he left the dog on his hind legs, to take care of the house.

"Reynard found the cat waiting for him. It was nearly dark when they came to the cave, but they could see the basket waiting for them; the fox assisted the poor little cat into it. 'There is only room for one,' said he; 'you must go first.' Up rose the basket; the fox heard a piteous mew, and no more.

"'So much for the griffin's soup,' said he."

"Oh! what a cruel, wicked fellow!" said Willie, almost crying.

"Reynard waited for some time, when Miss Griffin, waving her claw from the window, said cheerfully: 'All's right, my dear Reynard, my papa has eaten his soup, and is now sound asleep: forty cannons going off at once, would not wake him till he has slept off the boiled cat. Come and help me to pack up; I should be sorry to leave a single diamond behind.'

"'So should I,' said the fox. 'Why! the door is shut! open it, beautiful creature, to your adorer.'

"'Alas! my father has the key, you must come up by the basket; I will let it down for you.'

"The fox did not like much to get into a basket, that had taken his lady-love to be boiled, but the most cautious grow rash when money's to be gained: and avarice can trap even a fox. So he jumped into the basket, and went up in an instant. It rested just before it reached the window, and the fox felt, with a slight shudder, the claw of the hideous creature stroking his back.

71

"'Oh! what a beautiful coat,' said she, caressingly.

"'You are too kind,' said the fox; 'you can feel it better when I am once up. Make haste, I beseech you!'

"'O! what a beautiful bushy tail. Never did I see any thing like it.'

"'It is entirely at your service, sweet creature,' said the fox, 'but pray let me in.'

"'Really, such a beautiful tail; I don't wonder you are proud of it.'

"'Ah! my beloved Miss Griffin, you flatter me, but you pinch my tail a little too hard.'

"Scarce had he said this, when down dropped the basket, but not with the fox in it; he was caught by the tail, and hanging half way down, by the help of the very same sort of pulley with which he had cheated the dog. You may imagine his consternation; he yelped out, at a terrible rate—for it hurts a fox exceedingly to be hanged by his tail, with his head down—when what do you think happened? Why, the door opened, and out stalked the griffin, smoking his pipe, and with him, a fashionable crowd of all the beasts in the neighborhood.

"'Hallo, brother!' said Bruin, the bear, laughing fit to kill himself; 'whoever saw a fox hanged by the tail before?'

"'You'll have need of a physician,' said Doctor Ape.

"'Don't stay there to oblige us,' said Gauntgrim, the wolf.

"'A pretty match, indeed! Miss Griffin, for such as you,' said the goat, strutting by him.

"The fox grinned with pain, and said nothing. But that which hurt him most, was the compassion of a dull booby of a donkey, who assured him, with great gravity, that he saw nothing to laugh at in his situation.

"'At all events,' said the fox, at last, 'cheated and betrayed as I am, I have played the same trick on the dog; go laugh at him, gentlemen.'

"'Excuse me,' said the griffin, 'WE NEVER LAUGH AT THE HONEST.'

"'And see,' said the bear, 'here he is.'

"And indeed Beppo, after much effort, had gnawed the string in two, and freed his paw; the scent of the fox had enabled him to track him, and here he arrived, burning for vengeance, and finding himself already avenged.

"But his first thought was for his dear cousin. 'Ah! where is she?' he cried;

'without doubt that rascal Reynard has served her some trick.'

"'I fear so, my old friend,' answered the griffin; 'but don't fret. After all she was nothing particular. You shall marry my daughter, and succeed to all the treasure and all the bones that you once guarded so faithfully.'

"'Oh, no, no!' said the faithful fellow; 'I want none of your treasure, and, though I don't mean to be rude, your daughter may go to Guinea; I will run over the whole world, but I will find my dear cousin.'

"'See her, then,' said the griffin, and the beautiful cat, more beautiful than ever, rushed out of the cavern, and threw herself into the dog's paws.

"It was all over with the fox; the cat might forgive some things, but to be boiled alive for the griffin's soup—never!

"'And now, Mr. Reynard,' said the griffin, 'I wish you to understand that I have no daughter; it was me you made love to. Knowing what a tremendous tell-tale the magpie was, I amused myself with cheating her; quite a fashionable amusement—don't you think so?'

"The fox made a dreadful struggle, and leaped on the ground, leaving his tail behind him. It did not grow again in a hurry.

"'Sir,' said the griffin, as the beasts all roared with laughter at the comical figure Reynard made, running into the wood, 'the dog has beaten the fox, cunning as he is. Truth and honesty always come out right in the end.'

"You may be sure that Beppo was very soon married to his beautiful cousin the cat, and though dogs and cats, as a general thing, seldom live happily together, these two proved an exception, and lived to a good old age in perfect harmony."

"Oh! what a delightful story!" said Willie; "I wish you would read it all over again; how glad I am the wicked fox was punished at last; and, mamma, how mean it is to cheat! I intend to be like General Washington, I will never tell a lie, or cheat anybody, not even a dog or a cat."

"I hope and pray that you never will, my little son," said his mother; "I pity those poor children who are afraid to speak the truth; they don't consider that one fault leads to many more. I think even this story will show all who read it how much they lose by acting like Reynard the fox, and, if they are sensible, they will not despise the example of Beppo the dog, but resolve, after this, never to do a mean thing, and never to tell a lie. But come, Willie, I see your father at the gate; let us run a race, and see which will get to him first."

Willie sprang up, joyfully, and his mother and he stepped out of the window and, with a "one for good measure, two to show, three to make ready, and four to g-o-o,"—off they started, Willie's little legs clearing the ground in fine style, and, to his great delight, he won the race by about five yards, and rushed up to his father, such a laughing, breathless, handsome little fellow, that his father did what no father could help doing, caught him up in his arms and gave him a dozen good kisses, and then carried him back.

At the tea-table Willie told the story of the fox and the dog. I wish you could have seen his face, as the different incidents of the tale altered the expression; it was a perfect and most beautiful changing picture, and his father enjoyed his speaking face exceedingly, and exchanged many glances of delight and sympathy with his mother. The story became so great a favorite, that it was very often repeated, and Willie declares if ever he is tempted to do any thing mean, one thought of the good Beppo will be enough to shame him out of it.

Dear little readers, will you not say the same? Willie is, like yourselves, a real child, now living. If you were to take a ride on Long Island, as far as Fort Hamilton, you would pass the pleasant country house where he lives; very likely he would be playing near the gate. Every one that passes, says: "Hollo, Willie;" or "There's my boy;" or "Here, Willie, catch this apple." It is always a pleasant word, for every one loves him dearly.

Perhaps it will be hard to conquer a bad habit, all at once; but if you keep on trying, it is really surprising, how easy it becomes, till at last, you would find it rather more difficult to be bad than good.

I have simplified and extended the story of the fox, which was written by a celebrated author for grown people, because I felt sorry that so good a story should not be read and enjoyed by those for whom my heart is so brimful of love—the children.

It is my firm belief, that if the time ever arrives, when the children shall all grow up good men and women, the millenium will have surely come; to bring that about, all the present parents and guardians must help the children to be good; and it is also my opinion, that good precepts, affectionately impressed, good examples set before them, the reading of good books—the Holy Bible first of all, and above all—will do more than whole forests of birch rods. I have never yet appealed to a child's honor in vain, or told stories, portraying noble qualities, without a good effect; and I hope never to write one that will cause a single regret, either in me or my readers.

Lightning Source UK Ltd.
Milton Keynes UK
UKHW011846170822
407466UK00002B/94